I0606663

A
Long Shadow

Julie Kendrick

A Long Shadow

This is a work of fiction. Events and characters described herein are imaginary and are not intended to refer to specific places or living persons. The opinions expressed in this manuscript are solely the opinions of the author and do not represent the opinions or thoughts of the publisher. The author has represented and warranted full ownership and/or legal right to publish all materials in this book.

This book may not be reproduced, transmitted, or stored in whole or in part by any means, including graphic, electronic, or mechanical without the express written consent of the publisher except in the case of brief quotations embodied in critical articles and reviews.

All rights reserved.

© 2025 Julie Kendrick

Cover photo, *Victorian Home* © 2025 Kendrick Photographic Imagery

ISBN 978-0-9976262-6-1

ALSO BY JULIE KENDRICK:

BRAMBLE MYSTERY SERIES

A Fatal Development

A Grave Matter

MUSIC MEMOIR

Music and Mischief: Life Among the Melodeers

Old sins cast long shadows.

—Agatha Christie, *A Pocket Full of Rye*

Chapter 1

January 1999

The final year of the century bared its teeth and growled. 1999 in the Midwest would not go gentle into that night. A blizzard on the second day of January added several paragraphs to record books with a snowfall of nearly 20 inches, accompanied by frigid temperatures. The snow fell in sheets and a brutal wind howled it into drifts obscuring the lower half of my windows. I'd like to say that I was toasty warm in my little cottage in Bramble. I'd like to say it, but I was not toasty warm. Not toasty. Not warm. There was no power—no heat, no light. The phones were out. Dripping faucets, turned on to prevent my pipes from freezing and bursting, beat a tattoo in the kitchen and bathrooms. The windows rattled with each blast of the wind that wailed outside. I didn't dare go out in this blizzard. Definitely the winter of my discontent.

My cat, Minerva, and I huddled under a pile of blankets on the couch in front of my living room fireplace, which gave off a feeble warmth. I wore my fleece robe over my warmest clothes, my feet cold despite being clad in thick wool socks. The day was darkening, and soon I would need to light my kerosene lamp, purchased years ago for its decorative charm. Pulling the blanket closer around me, I counted the number of logs remaining in the bin and tried to estimate how long it would be before I would need to feed the last one to the fire.

A vivid imagination is both a blessing and a curse. As I half-dozed on the couch, I conjured visions of "Middle-aged Woman and Her Cat Found Frozen" being the lead story of a television six o'clock news report, with the station's "film at ten" showing rescue teams wiping tears from their eyes as they chipped away at the four-foot-thick block of ice encasing our blue lifeless bodies. Well, okay, my blue body. Minerva's body wouldn't be noticeably blue, covered as she is in black and white fur. I had day-dreamed my way into a fine snit when I heard banging at my kitchen door.

The pounding continued. I gathered the blanket around me and padded into the kitchen. Minerva lost no time in curling up in the remaining warmth of the couch.

***

A few years ago, I left Chicago and my career as an investigative reporter for *The Journal-Times* and accepted a position as its syndicated advice columnist, Miss Polly—a far cry from my previous life as Meg Smyth, hard-hitting journalist on her way to a Pulitzer. When the violence of the city struck me personally, I moved into the small home my Grandma and Grandpa Rasmussen left me in Bramble, a midwestern town unfortunately named by its founders for the abundant buckthorn they mistook for decorative shrubs in need of a bit of pruning. The house was one of several known as "Cottage Row" along the shore of Prairie Lake, a small body of water carved out by a retreating glacier eons past. The quiet was just what I needed and I quickly grew to love the town, its pace, its people.

I also met Brad Trinder, who, like me, moved to a house in Cottage Row as a retreat from his busy work life. He's a forensic accountant with the FBI— which sounds both exciting and dull. Exciting because it is, after all, the FBI, and dull, considering the stereotypical image of geeky, pencil-necked accountants. There aren't many wildly exciting moments when fraud or other dishonest endeavors are uncovered by FBI accountants. But Brad? Dull? Well, let's just say he doesn't own a pocket protector or green eyeshade.

***

And it was Brad at my door. As I peered through the frost-covered window in the door, only Brad's eyes were visible between the wool cap pulled down around his ears and a thick maroon wool scarf wrapped around his mouth and nose. Even the colors of his parka and gloves were hard to identify with so much snow covering them. His breath came in puffs and almost froze in the air. I tried to open the door, but it was frozen shut. Brad pushed as I pulled, and it finally opened with a screech. He stomped his feet on the mat inside the door, but didn't step all the way into the house.

"Am I glad to see you!" I said. "I thought you were working in Chicago today."

"I was. I managed to get a train home but had to leave my car at the Bramble station. They hadn't plowed the parking lot yet, so I walked home. I tried to phone you, but the lines are down, so I came over to check on you."

"Come in, come in!"

"I'll stand just inside the door, Meg. I don't want to drip all over your floor. Get some stuff together and come with me to my house where it's warm. Bring Minerva too. I'll scrape off the snow on your door frame so we can close it on our way out."

"Warm?" I willed my teeth not to chatter. "You have electricity and heat at your house? It's been out for hours."

"I put in a natural gas generator when I moved here. It doesn't serve the entire house, but the furnace, refrigerator, stove, and a couple of outlets work."

I got Minerva's carrier and some of her food, along with one of the disposable litter pans I kept on hand. I closed the fireplace glass doors in the living room, went upstairs and gathered up some clothes and put them in a couple of plastic trash bags rather than pulling out a suitcase from my closet. Brad took the bags and cat things while I grabbed Minerva and, over her truculent protests, stuffed her unceremoniously into the carrier. With my layers of clothes and my parka, I was like a gingerbread man, unable to bend my arms. As we clumped down the street to Brad's cottage, we walked backward to counter the wind whipping off Prairie Lake and peppering our faces with needles of ice.

After what seemed like an expedition through the Arctic, we reached Brad's. Inside, we removed our snow-covered coats, boots, and other outerwear and carried them into the bathroom where the snow on them would melt into the shower and tub. I released Minerva, who slunk close to the floor as she prowled the house.

"Wow!" I said, "What a storm. Thank you so much for rescuing me. I was truly snowed in."

"Come over here and sit down," he motioned to an overstuffed chair and ottoman in front of the fire. He brought over a wool stadium blanket bearing a University of Maryland terrapin logo and arranged it around me, then took my stocking feet in his hands and rubbed them. "Your feet are like blocks of ice." I refrained from sharing my earlier imaginings.

***

The following day was one of those crisp, blue and white winter days when snow crunched underfoot and ice clung to the trees in sparkles of silver. The power was still off, but thanks to Brad's generator, we were able to make scrambled eggs and bacon. We carried our breakfast and coffee into the living room, where we sat on the sofa and ate from trays in front of the fire. Minerva had already commandeered the single comfy chair and was sound asleep in one of those cat positions that can't possibly be comfortable.

"I wonder how your neighbors, Dr. Cam and Willow Podolski, did last night, with the snow and all," said Brad. "With Willow pregnant, we should probably check on them when we're finished with breakfast."

"Fortunately, they are not home. They decided to take the train into Chicago and spend New Year's Eve in the city at the Swissôtel. They were planning to come home today, but with the trains delayed and all, I imagine they'll stay another night in the hotel."

"Good," Brad replied. He got up and stretched. "I suppose I should go out and start shoveling."

"I'll help. It'll go faster. We can do the Podolski drive too. Being from Jamaica, they don't have much experience with snow. I wonder if they even have a snow shovel."

We bundled up and worked on Brad's driveway first, then trudged over to my house and began clearing my drive. We finished up at my house, shoveled the Podolski drive, and started back to Brad's house. As we leaned our shovels against his porch rail and stomped snow from our boots, the snow plow came rumbling down the street.

"Oh no!" we cried out in unison and reached for our shovels as the yellow behemoth deposited enormous boulders of snow and ice at the end of the driveways.

***

Power in Bramble was restored after another day. Although the temperatures still dipped well below zero at night, the sun was out every day. I was back in my house and running a load of clothes in the laundry area adjoining my kitchen when I heard grinding sounds coming from the lake. I looked out and saw the back end of my neighbors' new SUV protruding from one of the huge snow banks on the lake, several feet from the shore where the plows had pushed snow and gunk from the streets. My next-door neighbor, Willow Podolski, a heavy coat over her shoulders, stood on her porch, wringing her hands as she watched her husband climb out of the car.

I threw on my parka and boots, and picked my way over the snow to her. "What happened?" I asked.

"Oh, Meg, it's my foolish husband," she said. Her delicate facial features and traces of a soft Jamaican lilt in her speech were at odds with her irritation. "He's a gifted surgeon, lots of honors. But common sense?" She shook her head. "Over and over, Cam watched that movie, *Cool Runnings,* about the Jamaican bobsled team in the Olympics. I often wonder if that was one of the attractions about moving here, except instead of bobsledding, he thought he'd take up ice-skating. He doesn't know how to skate. But he bought a pair of skates and some hockey things and went out to clear some of the snow on the lake with the plow he bought for the front of the car. He doesn't know how to work the four-wheel drive. I told him he should read the manual first, but…"

"Not to worry, I'll go back home and call Bert Schmidt. He owns the local garage and has a tow chain he can hook up to his truck and pull Cam out." Or so I hoped. I wondered if there was a word for "tenderfoot" that applied to newbies in a Midwest winter. Or if any man reads manuals.

"Oh, no," said Willow. "Come inside and phone the man."

I removed my boots and gloves inside the door. The inside of the Podolski home was charming. Bright colors and a variety of pillows—even a few shaped like mushrooms—were scattered through the room. They had brought Jamaica with them.

After talking with Bert, I rejoined Willow on the porch. I remarked to myself what a handsome couple he and Willow made. Lovely light-brown skin that no amount of sun-bathing by Caucasians could hope to achieve.

Bert soon arrived and took charge. As he climbed out of his truck, he drew on well-worn, thick leather gloves over his driving gloves. He was dressed in brown Carhartt overalls and jacket with its collar turned up, and a knit cap bearing a patch reading "Bert's Garage" was pulled down over his ears. His face was red with cold and he stomped his feet to warm them; this job was not his first of the day.

The men talked as Bert got his towing gear ready. "I'll get you out in a minute or two, Doctor Cam," he said. "How did this happen?"

"Um…I thought I'd try ice-skating and I needed to clear the snow off the lake. Ice is thick underneath."

"Skate a lot in Jamaica, did you?" Bert grinned.

Cam grinned back and shook his head. "Not very much."

After a few minutes, Cam's car stood on dry land with globs of ice and snow clinging to it. Bert and I exchanged glances as Cam tried to start it. Silence.

After several more tries, Bert asked, "So, Doc, where do you want this towed?"

"I bought the car at the Toyota dealer in Walnut Creek. Needed an SUV, with the baby on its way and my mother coming here to help."

"I know where it is. I can tow it there."

"What do I owe you?" Cam asked.

"You don't owe me anything this time," Bert said. "Consider it a Welcome to Bramble gift."

Bert and Cam drove off in the tow truck, with Willow following in her car. I picked up Cam's brand-new hockey skates, stick, and a couple of pucks and placed them on the Podolskis' porch.

***

A few days after the episode, which I couldn't help thinking of as *The Jamaican Zamboni Incident,* I heard voices outside and went to the window. Although I couldn't hear exactly what was being said without opening the window, I saw Cam Podolski struggling with a battered valise and several enormous straw bags woven in bright colors. An older woman—presumably his mother from Jamaica come to help with their baby due in a few weeks—stood in their driveway. A tiny, bird-like woman, she fluttered her hands as she gave instructions to him. Willow stood at their door, holding it open. I was tempted to go outside and help with the bags, but decided Cam had enough to do with two women giving him directions.

Later that day, I dropped by to introduce myself. Cam opened the door. "Oh, hi, Meg. Thank you again for calling Bert for us the other day."

"How's the car?"

"Not anything that a good drying out and replacing the bolts on my plow attachment won't fix. Maybe a couple of parts for the bumper. I can pick it up tomorrow." He lowered his voice as he took my coat. "We told my mother the car was just in for regular servicing."

Making no reply, I bent to take off my boots and noticed the hockey skates in a corner of the hallway. His eyes following my glance, Cam said, "Won't be using these for a while," and quickly picked them up and shoved them into the closet, closing the door just as Willow and the older woman came up to us.

"Hi, Willow!" I said. "And, Cam, this must be your mom." I turned to her. "Hello. I'm Meg Smyth from next door. Welcome to Bramble!"

"Hello. Yes, I am Mrs. Podolski—the elder, of course. As you are a good friend of my son," she drew herself regally to her full height of almost five feet and said, "you may call me by my given name, Irie."

Chapter 2

February 1999

April is the cruelest month, according to T.S. Eliot. I concede his point of view, but I vote February as the brownest month. From my kitchen window, as I rinsed out my coffee cup, I could see the lake, thick with melting ice, undulating sluggishly while a few disconsolate Canada geese pecked at patches of dead grass around dirt-flecked snow piles of snow. I stroked Minerva as she rubbed against me.

Chill and gloomy though the weather was, I needed to run some errands, so climbed into my car and drove into town. I parked in front of the Bramble post office where I mailed some letters. Although the air was heavy and damp with a portent of snow, I decided to walk to Norton's Drugs and Sundries for breakfast.

I looked across the street at the once-beautiful Victorian home partially gutted by a fire several months before. A wave of sadness washed over me as I gazed at the dark ruin, bleak and abandoned, the chimneys of its blackened skeleton reaching ragged fingers to the sky. Behind a chain-link fence, charred boards and other detritus protruded from the top of a dumpster in the driveway. Yellow plastic tape fastened across the front door added the sole spot of color and flapped with each gust of wind.

The owner had bequeathed the property, formerly the Memory Gardens Funeral Home, to the village. Structural engineers declared the lower floor of the house safe, but a lot more work was needed before the entire building could be used. Suggestions poured in from Bramble citizenry. Town meetings were held and the village board met countless times to consider the ideas. Its decision was to be announced later today. I continued on to Norton's where I knew Mayor Fred Koenig and his cronies met for breakfast nearly every morning. Perhaps I could get an advance copy of the special pamphlet due to be distributed to homes and businesses. Or try to coax Hizzoner to give out some information.

As I entered Norton's, the store's warmth and the smell of fresh coffee and bacon greeted me like old friends. Although the summer season was still months away, the store's shelves were almost filled with towels, plastic sand shovels, and tanning lotions to attract the "weekend people" who drove out from the city to enjoy the public beach. I looked around for Phil Norton, the owner.

"Hi, Meg," said Phil, standing up from behind a floor display advertising Coppertone suntan lotion. His thick glasses gave him a look of a giant insect. He had confided in me that he had been diagnosed with macular degeneration.

Startled, I said, "Phil! I didn't see you there."

"One of the disadvantages of being short," he laughed. He gestured to the life-sized advertisement showing a smiling youngster whose tanned skin contrasted with his white bottom exposed by a playful dog tugging on his shorts. "That kid is almost as tall as I am."

"Still winter outside, but I guess it won't be long until the summer folks arrive," I commented, gazing at the shelves.

"Yeah. Good for business, but in many ways, I enjoy the off-season more. Get a chance to chat with people who live here. Slower pace too."

"I know what you mean," I replied, thankful I lived on the lake and didn't need to weave my way around water toys, over-excited children, and tired, sunburned mothers at the town's beach. I could take a swim or paddle my canoe around the lake whenever I was in the mood.

"Did you come in for a coffee to go, Meg?" When work started on the project across the street, Phil had installed a small pour-it-yourself coffee bar across from the cash register, pairing the java needs of the men with an additional source of income for Norton's. In a bit of clever marketing, the beverage cups had sayings about coffee printed on them—"A Yawn Is a Silent Scream for Coffee," "Seven Days Without Coffee Makes One Weak," "When Life Gives You Lemons, Trade Them for Coffee," and the like.

"Not this time, Phil. I'm here for breakfast. Your coffee counter is such a creative idea."

"Thanks, Meg. And it really is self-service. Just keep the urns filled. Honor system for the price, so I'm not tied up making change all day." He smiled. "Got that idea from Pastor Joe at the Lutheran Church. Said the church brings in more people for their potluck suppers with a free-will offering than if they charged a set price."

"That's my church, and he's right. And also, people without the means to pay can pay what they can afford. Or nothing at all."

"Yeah. I think some of Arch's workmen are a little short of cash just before payday, so that works for them, and I'm not losing money on the coffee set up. If they haven't paid for their coffee, they almost always make it up the next time they come in. I don't keep track.

"In fact, I'm thinking of adding espresso drinks, if I can find the room in here and someone—baristas they're called—to run the machine. That's the latest thing, lots of coffee houses popping up, although I can't imagine anyone paying three dollars for a cup of coffee. The only place I know of in Bramble that serves espresso is The Heron. And that's with dessert."

"You know, a few years ago, I couldn't imagine buying bottled water," I said, pointing to the rows of plastic bottles of water in the cooler. "Who would buy water? And yet, now I almost always have a few bottles in my refrigerator. Easy to take along water in the car or to the summer outdoor concerts." I turned to walk to the back of the store. "Enjoy the day, Phil."

I walked slowly past the wall of faded photos of Bramble history: the town's early days as an art colony just before World War Two, followed by photos of long-forgotten village luminaries—the local Red Cross women volunteers, seated, their legs crossed demurely, and the all-male village board who stood with hands clasped in front of themselves like a soccer team bracing for a penalty shot. In pride of place was a color photo of last year's Bramble High School football team, which had made it to the state finals. The players were arranged on bleachers in the order of their jersey numbers. I smiled as I imagined how long that took to organize. Like herding goldfish.

The clinking of silverware and china and the hum of conversation grew louder as I neared the luncheonette area. Faded posters advertising Green River and cherry phosphates decorated the walls around the counter, its chrome stools covered in green vinyl cracked and worn with years of use. Small bits of foam stuffing protruded from the silver duct tape patches.

Seated at their usual table, Fred Koenig and his friends were eating their daily high-calorie breakfasts, defying cholesterol with every mouthful. Fred looked up from his overflowing plate. "Hey, Meg!" he called. "Come on over and join us."

"If you're sure I'm not interrupting anything…" I said.

Pete Winters, owner of Pump N Dump septic tank service, replied, "Nah. Have a seat."

Bert Schmidt brought over a chair from the next table for me. "Good to see you, Meg. How's Bramble's Bobby Hull? Trying out for the Blackhawks?"

I laughed. "I don't think Dr. Cam's been out on the ice again. His wife would kill him." And if she didn't, I suspected his mother would.

"Come on over to the station—free car wash with a fill up this week."

"Thanks, Bert. I'll keep your offer in mind. My Celica needs it. All that salt and winter crud."

A waitress bearing two coffee pitchers came up to our table. Evidently, the goth look was staging a comeback. The young woman who stood at our table—hair too dark to be its natural color, dark lipstick and eye makeup, black fingernail polish—could be an offspring of Theda Bara and Bela Lugosi.

"What'll you have, ma'am?" she flicked an inquiring gaze at me as she turned over an empty cup, its glaze alligatored with age.

"Just regular coffee, thanks." I smiled at the "ma'am," thinking only older women were addressed that way. Get a grip, Meg, you *are* an older woman. Theda Bara? Bela Lugosi? Would this young woman even know who they were?

"Sugar and cream are on the table."

"I don't remember seeing you before. I'm Meg Smyth."

"I'm Sage Fletcher. Working here for a while until school starts in the fall."

I smiled and nodded. "Sage. Pretty name."

"Yeah, I guess. Could be worse. I have a cousin—a girl. Her parents named her Sequoia, if you can believe it."

I shook my head. "Where are you going to school?"

"Art Institute of Chicago. I got a scholarship there."

"Wow, that's great, Sage."

"Found a couple of roommates. So expensive to live in the city."

"Sure is. I lived there most of my life before coming here." I would've said more, but there were more customers coming in. "I'd best let you get back to work."

Sage nodded and walked quickly toward the kitchen, leaving me to ponder how parents can look at an infant cooing in her cradle and name her "Sequoia."

"Good to see you guys," I said to the group around the table.

"We're just discussing what's gonna happen to the old building across the street," said Jake Tigran, his usual greasy red baseball cap perched on his head. "Being in the plumbing business, I know those old copper pipes would bring a good price. I have a couple of sources…"

"It looks so sad," I said. "but I'd hate to see it torn down."

"Yeah," agreed Pete Winters, stirring sugar into his coffee. "Wallace Arnhart offered to anchor a small mall with his store. I'm hoping that they'll convert the site for several Bramble stores, you know, like Water Tower Place on Michigan Avenue in Chicago."

A vision of the upscale shops of Water Tower Place sharing space with Johnny's Bait Emporium flashed through my mind. I suppressed a chuckle.

"So, Fred, can you give us a hint about what's going to be done?" asked Bert.

"Well," said Mayor Koenig, wiping his mouth. "Just between us…" he said as he bent over the table as much as his girth allowed and took a deep breath. We leaned toward him.

"There you are! I might know you'd be in here." Fred's wife, Frieda, her matronly body encased in a severely tailored brown suit and her steel-gray hair gathered in a bun from which no wisps of hair dared escape, marched up to her husband. She acknowledged the rest of us with a glare, her thick dark brows drawn into a scowl. "The paper's going to be delivered in a few minutes, Fred, and your pager is turned off. Again." She curled her lip as she gave his plate a poisonous look. "And what is that you're eating? You know what the doctor said."

Fred, his florid complexion deepening to puce, removed the paper napkin serving ineffectually as his bib and looked at us. "Guess I'd best be going. Don't want to keep my sweetie pie waiting."

I busied myself stirring cream into my coffee, as I strained to keep my eyes from rolling at the idea of the authoritative Frieda Koenig, who also served *pro bono* as Bramble's village attorney, being anyone's "sweetie pie." Fred and Frieda—referred to by villagers as Freddy Squared behind their backs—made for the exit, Fred bowling along as he sought to keep up with the long, purposeful strides of his wife.

Our group watched them leave without comment. I didn't have the audacity to say a word, lest I snicker. Keeping my eye rolling in check was difficult enough. Thank goodness my eyeballs don't bump into each other and clang.

"Er, well," said Jake, filling in the awkward silence. "I'd better be going. Got to look at a couple of leaky pipes over at the Catholic church."

The men pushed back their chairs and left, but I lingered over my coffee. Like the others, I was eager to know the decision about the prime piece of real estate on Main Street. I had three choices: dawdle at Norton's until a bundle of *The Bramble Buzz* special edition containing the announcement brochure was delivered; go home and wait for my copy of the newspaper to be tossed into the front bushes; or camp out at the Town Hall and snag a copy. I paid my bill, shrugged into my coat, walked back to my car, and drove over to the Town Hall.

Chapter 3

Bramble's seat of government was located in a building of indeterminate style, with several additions cobbled on over the years, obliterating whatever architectural integrity the original structure may have possessed. As I entered the building, I admired, as always, the few surviving Art Deco touches: chandeliers of art glass and brushed nickel fixtures. Millie Pullen, a woman whose drab appearance reflected the building's exterior, had served as receptionist from time immemorial. She looked up from her work, her brows drawn together in a scowl. "Can I help you, Meg?"

"I came by to get a copy of *The Bramble Buzz.*"

"They'll be delivered to everyone's home this afternoon," Millie snapped, her face filled with annoyance. If Millie were weather, the forecast would never vary—cold and cloudy with a chance of drizzle.

"Yes, I know, but they're going to be available here soon with the announcement about future of the property of Main Street, right?"

"Not yet." She nodded toward the hallway leading to the offices. "They're looking over the copies now." She scowled. "Don't know why they didn't proofread them before they were printed," she huffed.

"I'll wait," I said, walking over to a small group of metal folding chairs.

I perused the bulletin board containing notices of upcoming committee meetings, a used clothing drive sponsored by the Girl Scouts, and other community happenings. A large poster appealing for entries for this year's Bramble Ramble 5K run dominated the collection. I mused about the coming of the 21st century. The year 2000 always had seemed distant, the future era when science-fiction stories were set. And yet, here we were, already in 1999…

My thoughts were interrupted by strident voices coming from Mayor Koenig's office down the hall. "You had one job, Fred, one job."

"Sugar plum…"

"Don't you 'sugar plum' me!" came Frieda Koenig's voice. "You were supposed to contact her about chairing the project." One of them closed the door and I heard no more.

A few minutes later, the two came out, each carrying an armload of newspapers, which they plunked down in the center of the reception desk. Millie glowered at the invasion of her workspace, but said nothing. Fred nodded at me, then scuttled back to his office.

Coming over to me, Frieda said, "Why, hello again, Margrethe." She was one of the few people who called me by my full name—which I shared with Queen Margrethe II of Denmark—even using the Danish pronunciation (MarGRAYtuh). "I have a favor to ask of you." She mustered a smile almost rusted from disuse as she fished a brochure from one of the newspapers. "We, um, encountered a bit of difficulty with the announcement about the property on Main Street."

***

Sally Montrose opened the door to her home. "Come on in, Meg," she said. "Happy to have the company on such a gloomy day." Sally was my best friend and sidekick since I moved to Bramble. She was the head librarian of the Bramble Library and we shared a love of books, bemoaned the decline of the English language, and discussed such arcane topics as the Oxford comma. She was dressed in charcoal tweed slacks and a soft, gray cashmere sweater with a Hermès scarf knotted loosely at her neck. A perennial tomboy, I had worn my second-best jeans and a clean sweatshirt for my trip to town that day. As with all close friendships, appearances mattered not at all.

"Come on back to the kitchen and warm up," Sally said. "I'm making us some tea, and I just took some tea cakes from the oven."

"That sounds wonderful," I answered, never having seen a tea cake in my life. I took off my boots, hung my coat on the coat tree in the small hallway, and followed her through the downstairs rooms of the Victorian "painted lady" she and her husband Craig had painstakingly—and expensively—restored. Each time I visited, I marveled at the hand-printed wall coverings, carved furniture, and other features that were carefully chosen and placed with period authenticity while remaining inviting.

Her remodeled kitchen with its institutional appliances was vast, reflecting Sally's love of cooking and entertaining; yet like the rest of the house, was cozy and welcoming. Two settings with china plates, sterling, and linens were on the table in the nook overlooking the garden. A tiered glass serving dish held three or four different types of small cookies, presumably the tea cakes.

Sally removed a large tea kettle from the stove and poured hot water into a china teapot containing an infuser with tea leaves. "I thought we'd have Darjeeling today."

"Sounds good," I said, thinking of my open box of ancient Lipton tea bags at the back of one of my kitchen drawers.

Sally set the tea items on the table. "So what's new? How's Brad?" she asked.

"Fine," I said. "It's nice to have Brad around more, now that he's working out of Chicago and not based in Washington, D.C." I shook my head. "It's hard to get used to in some ways. I've been single all my life. Miss Independent, that's me."

"So…?"

"We're happy as we are right now. We haven't taken the big step of moving in together. We're just down the road from each other and, in any case, neither of us have enough room for another person. He's eligible for an early retirement option. As for the future, well, we'll see…" I stared at the tea things.

"What is it, Meg? You look…stricken. Something about Brad?"

"Uh, no." I pointed to the teapot. "That's a tea cozy, right?"

"Yes. It keeps the teapot hot. I have several. I picked up this one at a craft fair a few years ago. It's crocheted. Why?"

"Um, my Aunt Gae and Uncle Arvid—you know, my Mom's sister and her husband in Denmark—sent me a handmade one for Christmas. I don't own a teapot. Never needed one. I just boil a cup of water in the microwave, and dunk a teabag in it."

"If you like, I have another teapot somewhere you can have." She paused and searched my face. "That isn't the problem, is it?"

"Well, no. The cozy they sent is cute—red and white, with little Danish flags all over it. I, um, thought it was a hat."

Sally's eyes widened.

"I had Brad take a picture of me in it. And I mailed their thank-you note, with the photo, to them this morning. If I'd just procrastinated writing the note just another day…"

Sally, stalwart friend that she is, guffawed—her hearty laugh out of sync with her casual, yet elegant appearance. Tears stood in her eyes. "I'm sorry, Meg. It's just the visual—the hat…Danish flags…"

I tried to be indignant, but giggles overcame me. "It didn't fit well but I put that down to it being hand-made. And I thought they'd like to see me in it."

"I'm visualizing you as a sleeping garden cherub wearing red-and-white…"

"…flags of Denmark," I gasped.

Sally paused and wiped her eyes. "What are you going to do?"

"I'm hoping they'll get a kick out of it. For years, Mom has regaled them with stories about my cooking mishaps, so maybe they won't be too surprised. I just hope they're not offended."

"You could take one of my teapots home and take another photo with the pot covered with your cute cozy…" Sally suggested.

"I could mention how versatile their gift is."

"Not only for winter wear and teapots, but as a party head covering—a joyful alternative to lampshades."

"Stop! My stomach hurts from laughing," I said, reaching for a tea cake.

We sat in companionable silence, liberally interspersed with chuckles.

***

"Sally, I have a couple of copies of the brochure about the old Memory Gardens building with me." I said as I reached into my purse.

"Oh, good. *The Buzz* hasn't been delivered yet, and I've been curious about what was going to happen to that property. Frieda did a marvelous job working with the estate to get the title cleared so quickly, but some of those hearings at the Town Hall were pretty acrimonious."

"I also have a message for you from Frieda Koenig."

"Oh? Whatever about?"

"She wants you to chair a committee."

"A committee! What committee? I can't get too involved, what with the library. The spring books will be arriving any day. You were with her. Why didn't she ask you to chair whatever it is?"

"It was too late." I handed her the brochure. "It's on page three."

She read through it and looked up, aghast. "What in the world is the Millennium Arts Committee? And why is my name down as chairing it?"

"Fred Koenig was supposed to talk with you about it, but forgot. It's an art exhibition, a fund-raiser to restore the building as a community center. Part of this year's Bramble Heritage Week." I said. "You have to do it, Sally. You'd be wonderful."

"You've got to be kidding."

"Frieda said she'd have to chair it herself if you wouldn't do it."

"That would be fine with me."

"It's for a good cause. Think of that wonderful Victorian mansion as a community center: dances, receptions, maybe even a little theater. No one would participate on the committee with Frieda in charge. You know it would be all rules and regulations, by-laws, standing rules, policies, sergeants-at-arms…"

"I'm not happy being placed in this position by Freddy Squared," Sally said. She took a sip of her tea. "Although I would love to see theater, art exhibits, and the like in Bramble. I was so afraid that the building would be razed and turned into a strip mall." Sally looked at the brochure again. "Bramble Heritage Week is always scheduled the week of the Fourth of July. I guess I can get some Bramble High kids to help with the new books."

"So you'll do it?"

"I suppose so—but not alone." Her eyes danced. "Welcome to the Millennium Arts Committee, Madam Co-Chair."

"Oh no…"

"Oh yes," Sally said.

I grabbed another tea cake.

***

As I shut the door from my garage and entered the kitchen, Minerva turned her beautiful green eyes in my direction from her perch on the kitchen window sill. I hung up my coat and scarf on one of the pegs on the wall, kicked off my boots, and sat down at the table. I thrust my feet into my fleece-lined Androscoggin slippers and wiggled my toes in delight.

Minerva arched her back in a stretch, threaded her way around several items on the counter, jumped down, and landed with a thud next to me. I'm always amazed her landings are so hard and graceless. She wound herself around my legs and gave the piteous meow she'd perfected to indicate it was time to feed her. Only the center of her dish was empty, the rest of the food pushed to the edges. I went over to the pantry, grabbed a can of vile-smelling Feline Fiesta, which I called Feline Fester, and opened it. I had no sooner emptied it into her bowl than she tucked into it without the barest acknowledgment of gratitude.

I glanced at the clock. Brad was due to arrive for dinner soon. A quick look into the refrigerator showed nothing of interest, unless one is fond of condiments, soggy lettuce, and half-empty bottles of salad dressings of various vintages. A restaurant carry-out box toward the back surely had something mutating in it; I dropped it, unopened, into the garbage can.

"Hi, Meg!" came Brad's voice from the door.

"Hi, yourself," I went over to him, and reached up to give him a kiss. I brushed a lock of auburn hair from his forehead. "Do you know your auburn hair is like Ronald Reagan's and Michael Rennie's?"

"I know who Ronald Reagan is, but who's Michael Rennie?"

"You know. He was in *The Day the Earth Stood Still.*"

"About aliens."

"Yes, he tried to save our planet from certain death."

"Speaking of certain death, I hope you haven't fussed over dinner," Brad said, a smile tickling his mouth as he placed a large shopping bag on the table.

"Nicely played." I take a lot of kidding about my disinterest in things culinary. I gave an exaggerated sigh. "Oh, woe is I! I slaved over the hot stove all day preparing beef bourguignon."

"Some goodies from The Heron will just have to do."

"Great! And how are Jon and Louis? I haven't seen them for a while." Jon Dreher and Louis Briggs were my other next-door neighbors and owned The Heron, Bramble's only "white tablecloth" restaurant.

"They said to say hello."

"Such a nice couple, and their food…"

***

The sky, sullen all afternoon, suddenly released the rain from its bruised clouds. I walked over to my living room window. Raindrops slid down the window like tears. Brad came up behind me, rested his chin on the top of my head, and we gazed at the night sky torn with forks of lightning. Thunder rumbled in the distance and tree branches creaked as the wind screeched through them.

I closed the curtains and we retreated to the couch. I mentioned my new job as Sally's co-chair of the Millennium Arts Committee.

"So what are your duties?" Brad asked.

"I'm not sure. She's called a meeting of the committee for next week."

"She pulled me in too. I ran into Sally and Craig at The Heron, and she asked me to be the "finance guy" for it—you know, keep the books, make sure the money gets to the bank, and so forth. Shouldn't be too difficult, so I agreed." He turned to me and gave me a salacious wink. "And of course, I'd need to study the co-chair's figure from time to time…"

Chapter 4

The sound of voices greeted me as I pushed open the door to the conference room at the Bramble Town Hall for the initial meeting of the Millennium Arts Committee, already known around town by its acronym, MAC.

"Hi, Meg!" called Sally. She indicated a chair next to her. Brad was already seated on the other side of her and waved to me. I was surprised to see the dour Millie Pullen busying herself with a pad of paper and a collection of pencils and markers stuffed into a chipped mug with "Tommy Bartlett's Water Show" printed on it in faded lettering. Sally caught my look and gave a slight shrug.

As Sally called the meeting to order, Frieda Koenig strode in, clothed in a gun-metal gray gabardine suit—like a battleship in full sail, if battleships had sails. Sally motioned her to an empty chair at one side of the table, but Frieda declined, saying, "I just popped in to see if all was in order." I didn't dare look at Sally, who was one of the most organized persons I knew. With Sally in charge, everything was always in order.

"Frieda," Sally said, "was there something specific you had in mind?"

"As the chair of Bramble Heritage Week, I wanted to tell you I added my sister-in-law, Gladys, to your committee. She has some ideas about attracting local crafters."

As if on cue, Gladys Koenig entered, slightly out of breath. Tendrils of brownish hair straggled out from under a cloche hat as she struggled to remove her heavy mouton coat dyed the color of a tired avocado. "So sorry to be late, everyone. That husband of mine," she simpered, referring to Billy Koenig, Bramble's police chief, "always likes to sleep in until the last minute." I composed my face into what I hoped was a bland look. Whatever I was thinking usually played on my face. I wouldn't last long as a poker player.

"Good to see you," Sally said to Gladys. "Have a seat and we'll get started." She paused. "Unless there was something else, Frieda?"

"I don't think so, thank you." Frieda headed toward the door. "Let me know if I can be of any assistance."

Sally looked at the group. "You all have copies of the agenda, and Millie Pullen here from the mayor's staff will be taking minutes of our meetings." Millie attempted a sour smile.

"Let's take a minute and go around the table and tell everyone else what tasks you've accepted to make the Millennium Arts Festival a rousing success. Meg?"

I smiled and said, "I think my job description as co-chair, is 'other duties as assigned,' so I'll pass to Brad Trinder."

"Hi," said Brad, looking around the table. "I'm the finance chair and will be keeping track of the money going in and out of our account at the bank. I'll set up some forms and procedures to help things go smoothly in that department."

"We're grateful to have Brad with us," said Sally. "He has quite a bit of accounting experience."

Brad sent her a look of gratitude when she didn't add that he was with the FBI. He felt it put people off, like finding a shark doing laps in the backyard swimming pool.

Arch Donegal stood up, his large rugged frame topped with his head of thick red hair. "You all know me as the guy overseeing various construction projects here in town," said Arch. "I've been here a while, after I wandered down from Alaska where I worked on the pipe line. The new addition to the Lutheran church, which we've been working on, is finished, so looking ahead, we'll have time available to finish renovating the downstairs of the old Memory Gardens building in time for the Heritage Week festivities."

The group applauded.

"Wonderful news," said Kim Winters and introduced herself. Slim with her dark hair worn in a pony tail, she was Pete's wife and a nurse at Bramble Memorial Hospital. "Some of the nurses from Bramble Memorial have volunteered to staff a first-aid station at the beach, and I'll be helping out in the first-aid tent in the parking lot of the Arts Center. Along with Doctor Podolski." She turned to the dark-skinned man next to her.

"Most of you don't know me yet, unless you've sprained an ankle or broken a bone or two. I'm Cameron Podolski, but just call me Doctor Cam or just Cam. Either is okay. My wife, Willow, and I moved here from Jamaica a few months ago. We live next door to Meg," He smiled. "In case you're wondering, my Polish father came to Jamaica and fell in love with a Jamaican woman, so I don't look very Polish."

A good-natured chuckle rippled through the group.

"And you have a baby on the way. When is it due?" asked Kim.

"It won't be long now. My mother came up to help out. She's a midwife in Jamaica." Cam looked at the woman seated on the other side of him. "I should know your name, as I believe we've met…Doctor…"

"I'm Celeste Farnsworth," she said. "I'm kind of new here too. I'm head of the addiction wing at the Wellness Center in Walnut Creek." She fingered a string of pearls at the neck of her light lavender cashmere sweater. Her soft gray suit jacket was over the back of her chair. "Sally asked me to oversee the Arts Festival entries." She looked at Sally. "I see that the procedure is next on the agenda. Since everyone's been introduced, shall I go ahead and outline my plans?"

"Yes, please," replied Sally.

Celeste passed around several sheets of paper stapled together. "I'm not going to read these items to you. You can do that at your leisure, so I'll just summarize. We'll have a juried show with admissions determined by three of us: Arch Donegal here, who studied art before he turned to construction—and he agreed to show one of his smaller pieces from the University of Oregon's permanent collection. He's contacted the university about it."

Arch shrugged. "Glad to help."

"Also on the art jury are Meg in her capacity as co-chair, and myself."

Me? Evaluating art entries? Before I could process this bit of information, Gladys Koenig stood up and shouted, "No! That's terrible! This show needs to be for local crafters—not some la-di-da *artistes*!"

Beneath her necklace, blotches of color began dotting Celeste's neck as she struggled to keep her composure as she replied, "Gladys, this is an art exhibition. I don't have anything against homemade items, but this really isn't the venue for them."

"That's outrageous! It's for everyone! It's a *festival!*" Gladys retorted, her voice crackling with anger. She grasped the pencil she was holding so tightly it snapped in two. "I've talked to several crafters who are thrilled to have an opportunity to display and sell their work."

Thoughts of sweet little boxes made from tongue depressors by loving hands at home sprang to mind. I managed to push them from my thoughts and asked, "What kind of things do your friends make, Gladys?"

"Wonderful items: afghans, birdhouses, crocheted hats…"

I didn't dare look at Sally, who quickly suggested, "What if we have both a juried art show and a separate local crafts area?"

"That's okay with me," said Celeste.

"Me too, I guess," said Gladys, who resumed her seat and looked around in triumph. Her foes were vanquished.

"Would you be in charge of the crafts area, Gladys?" asked Sally.

"Of course," she said.

I detected an unexpressed sigh of relief around the table.

The meeting continued with no further squabbles, and adjourned an hour or so later.

As we made our way out of the room, Frieda Koenig came from her office and motioned to Brad,

"Brad! Do you have a few minutes? I have something to ask you."

"You go on, Meg, I'll catch up with you," he said.

"Me too, Meg," said Sally. "I'll just be a moment. Need to sort out my notes from the meeting."

I walked out with Millie, who groused about Frieda Koenig assigning her to take minutes at the committee meeting. "Like I got nothing else to do. And no extra pay neither."

I made an attempt to break through her unsociable demeanor and asked, "So how is Charlene doing?" Millie's daughter recently began work at the local beauty salon, Gloria's Glamour.

Millie brightened slightly. "She has some new guy she's dating. Seems nice. Maybe she'll settle down one of these days. She likes being at Gloria's and plans to take courses to be a beautician."

"She'd be good at that."

Millie returned to her saturnine persona. "Yeah. If it ever happens."

I sighed. With Millie, every silver lining has a cloud.

Chapter 5

Brad, Sally, and I had agreed to join Sally's husband, Craig, at the Prairie Palace Hotel after the meeting for the hotel bar's popular Happy Hour. I arrived first and picked out a table. Sammy, the bartender, hustled over. I was tempted to imbibe in one of his mixed drinks of remarkable potency, but decided on the house merlot.

A few minutes later, Craig Montrose entered, Sally on his arm. Dressed as usual in slacks and a tweed jacket, he looked over his eye glasses and attempted a Cagney-esque leer at his wife. "I met this good-lookin' chick outside and invited her in for a drink." I smiled as he helped Sally off with her coat and arranged it on the back of her chair before folding his tall, slim frame onto the chair next to it. "Hi, Meg," he said. "What're you drinking?"

"Just a glass of merlot. It's been a while since lunch and I didn't want to drink one of Sammy's specials on an empty stomach."

"I'll have the merlot, too," Sally said to Sammy, as he came up bearing a tray with an array of hors d'oeuvres, "although after that meeting, I need Prozac over ice." Sally reached for a stuffed mushroom wrapped in pastry. "Why did I agree to chair this?"

Brad came up to our table. "Hi, everyone." He shook Craig's hand, sat down, and took a swallow from the bottle of beer he'd picked up from the bar on his way in.

"What did Frieda want?" I asked Brad. "She seemed intense."

"Um, well…she asked me to be the treasurer of her election campaign."

"What!" we exclaimed. One or two other patrons glanced at us, then returned to their own conversations.

Sally said, "The whole town knows she running for mayor now that her husband Fred is retiring. Why does she need a campaign? She's running unopposed, right?"

"Well, no, actually, she isn't," Brad replied. "Someone else is running against her." He took a sip of his beer.

"Who?" we chorused. A few more customers looked over at us.

"You sound like a bunch of owls," Brad said.

"Actually, that would be a parliament of owls," said Craig in his pedantic way. "Evidently, someone thought owls reflected the wisdom of Parliament, and…"

Sally placed a gentle hand on her husband's arm before he could enlighten us about owls or parliaments. "Stop teasing us, Brad," she said.

"Wally."

"Who?" we asked, throwing caution to the wind and risking owls and parliaments. The number of other people staring at us was growing.

Brad took in our puzzled expressions. "I thought you'd all know who that is. He owns Bushel O'Bargains."

"Oh, Wallace Arnhart," I said. "Never knew him as Wally. He always referred to himself as Wallace, which matches his supercilious attitude and fake upper-crust accent. Mostly, I just run in for a few of his overpriced groceries or a bottle of wine. He's not much for nattering and chit-chat."

"Maybe he thinks Wally sounds more folksy," commented Sally. "Does he have a platform? I thought Frieda, with her experience, would be a shoo-in. And everyone knows her." She took a sip of her wine.

"She's not exactly lovable, but she certainly runs a tight ship."

"According to Frieda, Arnhart thinks the mayor of Bramble should be a man," replied Brad.

"What!" we exclaimed in unison. The people at other tables raised their heads again and I was reminded of those plastic birds that lower their heads up and down to sip water. By now, only the waiters and busboys refrained from giving us the stink-eye.

"Frieda is distributing her campaign buttons now," Brad said, and tossed a handful of them on the table. Sally picked one up and read, "The Best Man for Mayor in 2000 is a Woman!" She grinned. "So, Brad, you're her campaign manager? How disloyal to your gender!"

Brad tried, unsuccessfully, to look abashed.

"What's Arnhart thinking?" said Craig. "Is he aware that the Nineteenth Amendment was ratified almost eighty years ago?"

I thought of the photos on the wall in Norton's. "He's a throwback to another era."

"Maybe he didn't realize that Ira Levin's book, *The Stepford Wives,* was satirical," said Sally, ever the librarian.

"It was?" Brad asked in mock surprise. "I enjoyed the movie, got a lot of pointers," said Brad. He looked over at me.

"And how's that working for you?" I asked. We all laughed.

"In any case, I think we'd better get behind Frieda," Craig said, reaching for a campaign button. "Bramble would be taking a big step backward with Arnhart."

We raised our glasses in solidarity, clinked them together, raised them in a jovial salute to the roomful of exasperated customers, and shouted, "To Frieda!"

***

Brad and I walked back to our cars, which were parked near each other. A thick cloud cover had moved in and veiled the stars as a blustery wind scurried the few dry leaves autumn had left behind. By the time we reached my cottage, snow began to fall in earnest and the lake's surface was dark and forbidding.

We hung up our coats and Brad took his usual seat at the kitchen table "Brr. That wind is brutal," he said. "like daggers. Glad to be inside." Minerva, true to her species, didn't race to the door in high excitement to greet us, but as soon as Brad was seated, she jumped on his lap, circled a couple of times, and curled up.

I made some decaf coffee and we chatted about the upcoming election this fall. Mayoral elections in Bramble are held every four years, but unlike the most of the country, they take place in odd-numbered years. so terms of office begin in even-numbered years.

"I still can't believe you're Frieda Koenig's campaign manager. And the treasurer for Bramble Heritage Week."

"Frieda and Sally are difficult to refuse," Brad answered. "Besides, I want to put down roots in Bramble, get to know people." He looked over at me and reached for my hand. "I have no plans to leave here."

Neither of us said any more, but a flutter of excitement thrummed in my heart for a long time afterward.

Chapter 6

Next day, Brad had an early morning train to catch into the Loop for a meeting, so he'd gone back to his own house the night before. Minerva blinked at me. Stiff from sleeping all night curled around her, I swung my feet out of bed with the grace of a leviathan rising from the deep. I walked into the bathroom. Never missing a chance to share a bathroom moment with me, Minerva took a spot on the rim of the bathtub.

A quick glance in the mirror told me I needed a haircut. So annoying. Yesterday, my hair looked just right in the morning, and a few hours later, it was too long. And my gray hairs were no longer a sprinkling of silver threads among Miss Clairol's gold. Maybe I should visit Gloria's Glamour Salon and have my hair cut and colored. I could also treat myself to a pedicure before my toenails resembled a bird of prey's. I thought back to my last hair experience with Gloria. Maybe only the pedicure.

I took a shower, dressed, went downstairs, and fed Minerva. Some coffee and toast for me, and I started off for the Clipper Snip Barbershop. I've had my hair cut by a barber for years. It was quick and matched my hurry-up lifestyle when I lived in Chicago, and I had no reason not to continue that practice in Bramble. Besides, there were few more worthless pursuits than sitting under a dryer, reading out-of-date movie magazines about the activities of Hollywood studs and starlets referred to by their first names, but unknown to me.

I pulled up in front of the barbershop, managed to avoid wading in a puddle of brownish slush, and went in.

"Hi, Russ!"

"Hiya, Meg!" called out Russell Banks, the owner. "Take a chair. I'm almost finished with this guy."

"Hmmg!" said the man in the chair, his face swathed in hot towels. His uniform gave away his identity.

"Hi, Billy!" I called to Bramble's police chief.

The shop door opened and Pastor Joe Jenkins came in and wiped his feet on the mat inside the door.

"Pastor Joe! Good to see you," said Russ.

"It was time for a haircut," the pastor answered. "Gotta look good for Shrove Tuesday." Jenkins was pastor at the Bramble Lutheran Church.

"The Mardi Gras bash, right?" said Russ.

"Yep. Mardi Gras—French for Fat Tuesday," he replied. "A great day to celebrate the official opening of the new addition at the church. We've been using the space already, of course.

"I wouldn't say 'bash,' exactly," he continued, "but the church ladies will be making large batches of pancakes. Because the addition is primarily a youth center, our entertainment will be provided by young people. The Bramble High School glee club will perform and lead a sing-along." His eyes twinkled and an elfish grin stole across his plump face. "I wonder what songs the kids will select for us to sing along with them. Somehow, I don't think 'Bicycle Built for Two' or 'The Old Gray Mare' will be in their repertoire."

"Why pancakes?" asked Russ.

"Well, Lent starts the next day, Ash Wednesday. Shrove Tuesday is the last day to remove edible temptations like meat, eggs, and fats—as in pancakes—before being shriven by confessing one's sins, being forgiven, and assigned penance. Most of us don't follow that practice strictly today, but a lot of people give up something during Lent."

"Russ, you could use a few pancakes," I said, looking at his spare frame. "Maybe if I stand next to you, some of my calories would migrate to you."

Russ smiled. "I try to watch what I eat. Cardiac problems run in my family. Although I think I'll make an exception and come to the Mardi Gras thing."

I said, "I've seen signs all over town about the opening. I even saw posters in Walnut Creek when I was there last week."

"Yes," said the pastor. "The celebration is open to everyone—not just members of Bramble Lutheran. We're hoping the new addition will be more of a drop-in center for all kids. Give them things to do after school or evenings." He sighed. "Kids have so many ways to get into trouble these days."

"That's for sure," Chief Koenig said as Russ unwrapped his face. He threw back his shoulders and made a valiant attempt to suck in his stomach. "But don't worry. We enforce a strict curfew. The Bramble police force is on the alert."

Reluctantly, I denied myself yet another eye-rolling opportunity.

***

My hair wasn't much shorter when I left the barber-shop, but my neck felt naked as it always did after a haircut. Bushel O'Bargains was close by, so I left my car where I'd parked it and walked toward the gourmet grocery store. As I approached, I saw one of Wallace Arnhart's campaign posters on the light post in front of his store. His photo was embellished with long pigtails. Guess the curfew enforcement had skipped a beat. I tore off the poster and brought it into the store with me so I could throw it away.

Wallace Arnhart, his styled hair and goatee almost completely gray, stood to one side of the checkout counter. A frown topped his long, thin nose and his arms were crossed in front of him. I handed him the poster. "Not very nice," I said.

"No, it's not," he replied, glancing at the poster before tossing it into the wastebasket near him. "My 'worthy' opponent's work, I suppose. Dastardly."

The word hung in the air. Dastardly? Has anyone used that word since FDR's Pearl Harbor speech? Not to be linguistically outdone, I responded in kind. "I can't give credence to the idea that Frieda Koenig would be part of such an egregious act."

"Hmmph."

"What is your platform?" I asked.

"I wouldn't expect you to understand," he said, looking at me as if my ignorance was unsurpassed in the Western world.

My jaw tightened. Condescension is one of my hot buttons. If I could, I would summon a demon to deal with him. Not an ordinary, run-of-the-mill demon. Oh, no. Nothing less malevolent than Vlad the Impaler would do. I glared at Arnhart. "Try me."

"Very well. I'll make it simple for you. It's time for a man to be in charge."

"But Mayor Koenig *is* a man."

Arnhart snorted. "Everyone knows his wife is the one who runs things. Women have no place in government. Bramble is stuck in the mud, with stupid ideas like that artsy thing they're doing down the street. More shops would've been a boost to the economy. I even offered to anchor a strip mall with my store." He smirked. "That answer your question, *Ms.* Smyth?" he asked, sarcasm dripping. He turned away and busied himself behind the counter.

Discretion being the better part of valor, I swallowed several clever retorts. Tempted as I was to stomp off, I didn't want to leave the store immediately, lest I appear to be in retreat. Besides, the election coverage could be a small-town feature Chicago readers of *The Journal-Times* might be interested in, so best not to burn any bridges just yet. I let Arnhart have the last word and sauntered to the rear of the store. As I studied the various wines displayed, a familiar voice behind me said, "Hey, Meg! We haven't seen you for a while."

I turned. "Ben! And Nina! So good to see you!" I replied. I hugged them both. The Fultons were a welcome reminder that there were more people like them in the world than there were Wallace Arnharts. At least I hoped so. Ben and Nina were gray-haired, a bit plump, and always ready with a smile. They looked alike in that way that couples often do who are enjoying a long, happy marriage together.

"I haven't needed anything from your hardware store, Ben. For a change. A house built as a summer cottage is charming, but it seems there's always something to fix." I turned to Nina. "How are you, Nina?"

"Oh, the new physical therapy facility in Walnut Creek is doing wonders for me. I'm much more flexible and mobile now. And we both love having Sage Fletcher around. She's staying in the little apartment over our store, you know. Her grandpa was one of the students when Bramble was an artist colony, so she thought it would be fun to take a room at the hotel for a couple of days. When she discovered we had a room available and Phil Norton offered a job, she decided to stay until the start of the fall semester."

"My dad is at the Center for a while, too— therapy to strengthen his heart," I said.

"Oh? I'll look for him when I'm there," Nina said. "Are your parents still staying with you, Meg?"

"With Dad needing regular therapy almost every day, it made sense for them to stay in one of those apartments close to the facility. I visit as much as I can, and Mom rented a car, so the two of them come over once in a while."

"That's good. Do you think your folks will go back to Arizona?"

"I don't know," I replied. "All of his cardio doctors are in Chicago, so they may think of moving back here. Although they do hate the winter weather."

"They're not alone in that," said Ben. "At least, when it snows this late in the season, it doesn't stick or stay on the ground very long."

"Are you and Nina going to the grand opening of the church's new addition?"

"Wouldn't miss it. Besides, Nina is baking some of her wonderful cookies for it." He chuckled and patted his small paunch. "She says she'll hide them if I keep filching them."

"Speaking of which, I'd better finish shopping and get the spices we came in for," said Nina.

"So good seeing you," I said.

I watched them walk away, arm in arm. I pulled a bottle of New York claret from the shelf and tried not to gasp at the price. I put it back. There are limits to my discretionary valor.

I walked to front door and was relieved to see that Wallace Arnhart wasn't at the cash register—although I was ready with several snarky rejoinders for his arrogance. Sage Fletcher was ringing up items.

"Hi again, Sage. You're working here, too, I see."

"Oh, hi, um…"

"Meg Smyth. I met you at Norton's Drug Store the other morning."

"Oh, right." She looked at me through her caterpillar false eyelashes. "You were having breakfast with those elderly gentlemen."

Oh dear. I was older than several of those elderly gentlemen.

Chapter 7

I glanced at the clock on my dashboard. I still had some time before it would be dark, so I drove to the town hall to see Fred Koenig. In addition to my regular "Miss Polly's Opinion" advice column, I had an ongoing assignment to contribute to a "round-up" of how various communities in the paper's subscriber area were spending the last months of 1999, along with their plans to celebrate the year's odometer turning to 2000. When I asked if Mayor Koenig was in, Millie Pullen looked up from her filing, flashed me an annoyed look, and motioned me toward his office.

I rapped on his office door and heard the dull sound of his feet hitting the floor from their usual position propped on his desk.

"Come in," called the mayor. I entered as he was settling back in his chair. "Sit, sit, Meg. Always a pleasure to see you. How is our little journalist today?"

Little journalist indeed. Having had a crown replaced at my dentist's office a few weeks ago—the cost of which was enough to topple the economy of a small country—I resisted the urge to gnash my teeth. "Hi, Your Honor," I said. "I won't take up much of your time. I'm just following up on what the plans are for celebrating the millennium."

"Sure. Ask away," Koenig replied.

I leafed through my notes from my last interview with Hizzoner and decided to focus first on his plans for a parade. "Are you still planning a big parade on New Year's Eve?" I asked. "Might be a bit chilly."

"Um…well, I'm not sure whose idea that was, but, well…" He hemmed and hawed his way through a few more partial sentences. "We've narrowed it down to a big bonfire at the high school football field and fireworks." He lowered his voice. "Can you keep a secret?" I nodded. He gave me a wink. "Frieda thinks having fireworks is too expensive. She doesn't know that I'm going to buy the firecrackers when they go on sale right after July Fourth this year. I'm going to be first in line at one of those fireworks stores across the state line. We can store the stuff in that abandoned warehouse across the lake until New Year's Eve."

"Everyone likes fireworks," I said, and changed the subject. "So, Fred, what's this about Wallace Arnhart running for mayor?"

Fred scowled. "He's a jerk."

No news there. I probed Fred more. "He seems to be anti-women."

"Yeah. But really he's mad because we didn't go for his plan to have Bushels O'Bargains anchor a mini-mall. He's making all kinds of noise behind Frieda's back about there being something fishy about how quickly the estate was settled so work on it could begin."

"What's Frieda think about all this?"

"You probably should ask her," the mayor said, "but I gotta tell ya, the wife won't go down without a fight."

I sat up straighter. "What do you mean?"

Hizzoner said, "They're gonna have a debate, and she'll really nail him. She's so well prepared. Facts and figures. Charts." He snorted. "Arnhart doesn't have a chance."

When I got home, I dialed up America Online, listened to the annoying bangs, whistles, and squawks as it connected, and sent the latest "Miss Polly's Opinion" column to Harry Josten, my editor at *The Journal-Times*. Along with it, I sent a brief summary of what I'd learned so far about Bramble's election.

***

The pantry added nothing to my dinner menu and Brad was staying downtown. I went over to the wall phone and punched in the number for the local pizza parlor. I twirled the tangled coil of wire attached to the receiver as I gave my order: extra cheese, a variety of toppings, and no anchovies or pineapple. Did anyone get both anchovies and pineapple? One would be bad enough. And why are pizza joints called "pizza parlors?" Enough mental meanderings. My encounter with the Fultons reminded me that I should find out how Dad was doing with his therapy. As I was about to call and check on what hours he had therapy this week, the phone rang, and, as is sometimes the case, it was just the person I was about to call.

"Hi, Meg," said Mom. "I'm running a couple of errands tomorrow afternoon and thought I'd drop by and see you for a few minutes if you'll be home."

"Tomorrow afternoon would be good, Mom. I have a pedicure appointment in the morning. How's Dad doing?"

"He's fine. Amazing he gets any therapy done— he's always chatting with the staff there. They all love him, of course."

"Of course. Although they've probably learned more about millwork and cornices than they ever wanted to know."

I heard the smile in Mom's voice when she said, "No more talking now. We won't have anything more to say when I get there." As if.

Chapter 8

Gloria's Glamour was warm and humid, the air filled with the pungent odors of hairspray and permanent wave solution. Gloria Morelli, the owner, hastened over and looked pointedly at my head. Uh-oh. She must've seen me outside the Clipper Snip. "You really should have your hair cut by a trained, licensed beautician, Meg, not a barber. Salons are for women. Barbershops are for men who don't care about style."

I tried not to look at Gloria's head, covered as it was with ringlets of magenta, interspersed with highlights of vivid purple. "I'll think on it."

She consulted the calendar on the desk. "I see you're here for a pedicure," she said. Another pointed look, this time at my hands. "We could do a manicure while you're here, too."

I yielded. "Okay."

I walked to the rear of the shop where the foot baths were. All the stations were empty, and Charlene Pullen said, "Any seat will be okay, Meg. I'll do your fingernails too."

As she fussed about with various tools and towels, I asked how she liked working at the salon. "Oh, I love it," she replied, her smile spreading ear to ear. "I'm going to go to the beautician academy in a while. I'm putting money aside for it, and Gloria will match what I save up."

"Wonderful, Charlene," I said, thinking how different her manner was from her mother's austere mien. "And how generous of Gloria."

"She's really nice to work for," Charlene said. She lowered her voice. "I don't think this is public knowledge yet, but Gloria is Frieda Koenig's image consultant. You know, for the election."

I looked down at my feet so Charlene wouldn't notice my eyes rolling as far as they would go. Soon I would need larger sockets before my eyeballs pushed their way through my head and popped out the back.

***

When Mom arrived, I went out to her rented SUV to help her with the grocery bags she was bringing in. I don't believe she's ever visited me without bringing food. My Grandma and Grandpa Rasmussen had come to the States with their two small children, Mom and her sister, my Aunt Gae. Gae returned to Denmark and married, whereas Mom met Dad when she attended college in the States, and stayed here. She retired as an English teacher a few years ago at about the same time Dad sold his carpentry business.

Mom took off her coat and hat and smoothed her hair as I toted the bags to the kitchen.

"Mom, you must've bought out the grocery store!"

"Just a few things, dear," she said, as she joined me in front of the refrigerator. Peering inside, she said, "Margrethe Gae! What *do* you eat? If I shouted inside this refrigerator, my voice would echo."

I made no reply. Not after being addressed by my full name.

Mom took a seat at the kitchen table. "Your nails look nice, dear," she said.

"Thanks, Mom." I splayed out my fingers and admired them. "Every time I go into a beauty shop, the smell reminds me of the days when you used to torture me with those home permanents."

"They were just to give your hair—"

"—a little body." We both finished together.

I laughed. "I kept believing that my hair would be just like my best friend, Carol's." I sipped my coffee. "And then Dad would cut my string-straight bangs."

"And cut and cut," Mom added. "He kept trying to get them even and they got shorter and shorter."

"Always the day before school pictures were taken."

"You seemed to survived it okay," Mom said.

I walked over and squeezed her shoulder. "Survived and thrived. I had a great childhood and great parents."

Mom's eyes misted a bit, then widened when I told her Gloria Morelli was going to be Frieda Koenig's image consultant.

"I can't imagine what that might mean," Mom said. "Or look like."

"Guess we'll have to wait and find out at the debate with Arnhart," I said as I went over to the counter and started pouring her coffee. "Unless you'd rather have tea?" I asked.

"I'll stay with coffee," she replied, reaching for the mug, "although I've heard you have a nice new tea cozy." She gave me an insouciant look, but her chin quivered with the effort of holding in her laughter.

"Uh-oh. I take it you heard from Aunt Gae. I hope she's not too upset."

"Not at all! Your photo made my sister's day. Even your reserved Uncle Arvid laughed. She's shown it to all her friends. You and the tea cozy are the talk of Copenhagen!"

I took a gulp of my coffee. "By the way," I said in a desperate attempt to change the subject, but missing the mark entirely, "Our arts festival will have a crafts section, too."

"You could enter the tea cozy!" said Mom, not relinquishing the theme. "I mean, not to sell, of course. And they make pottery in the crafts room at the rehab center. Maybe your Dad could make a teapot for it…" I said nothing. When Mom got that look in her eyes and talked faster and faster, brooking no interruption, there was no stopping her.

I tried again to shift the topic, this time with more success. I handed her a flyer about the grand opening of the church addition. "Do you think you and Dad would like to go?"

"I assume you'll be going? With your man?"

I side-stepped the "your man" remark and said, "Absolutely. I think the whole town will be there. It's been a long winter, and I think people are excited to be getting out and seeing everyone."

"I'll try to get there. I'd like to see Pastor Joe and some of the friends I've made here. I'm not sure if your Dad will come. He has therapy in the morning and again in the afternoon, and he can hardly stay awake through dinner. His emphysema seems better, but he was running a slight fever today—not to worry—so don't count on us being there."

We sipped our coffee. "Mom," I asked, "what are your plans for when Dad finishes his therapy?"

"As you know, right now we're renting, month to month, one of the little apartments the rehab center has available for families. We think we'll sell our condo in Arizona and move back here. All of Dad's doctors are here, and, well, so are you...."

"Wow! That would be terrific!"

"We've become weary of apartment living, so I'm not sure what we'll decide. If we could find a one-floor house, that might be ideal. Not to worry—we don't plan to move in with you—one too many women in the house."

I tried not to show my relief at this latter remark. "There's a wonderful trailer park just off the Interstate. Residents are all over fifty-five."

"A trailer! Oh, Meg, I don't think so. I'd be afraid of my neighbors, even if they are older."

"It's really nice, Mom. It's landscaped, mature trees, a couple of little ponds where Dad could fish." I added, "Not what you think. Or see in movies. No one's been found cooking crystal meth. And the serial killers living there have dwindled in number."

Mom smiled and shook her head. "I don't know, Meg. Maybe. It's a while yet before we have to make a decision, so…"

I saw Mom out, and as I started to close the door, Mom wriggled her hand in greeting to Willow and her mother-in-law in their yard and walked over to them. I didn't have a coat on, so I leaned against my doorway and watched.

Irie was pointing out various parts of the flower beds to Willow. They both straightened up as Mom approached. The three women greeted each other and chatted. After a while, Mom nodded to the two women and walked back to me. Irie returned to whatever she was concerned about in the borders. Willow stood, silent and rigid, as Irie emphasized her remarks with dramatic gestures.

I motioned Mom back inside. "So you've met Cam's mother," I said.

"Yes. She told me to call her by her given name. Such an imperious manner. I didn't know if I should curtsy or genuflect!"

"What was all the conversation about?" I asked. "It looked like Willow was getting the worst of it."

"Something about what kind of bulbs and perennials were in the ground. That poor girl. She didn't know what had been planted by the previous owner. She can't do anything right, according to her mother-in-law."

"They just moved here in November, so they won't know what flowers are there for a few weeks yet. The house has been empty for a long time, so I don't remember what bloomed there either." I laughed. "Perhaps Willow should plant mother-in-law tongues."

"As I said before, too many women in one house. I asked Irie if her name means something special in Jamaican." Mom started laughing, and gasped, "It means…it means 'One Who Spreads Harmony.'"

Chapter 9

Mardi Gras, February 1999

The new fellowship hall at Bramble Lutheran thumped with music from huge speakers and pulsed with swirling strobe lights. Conversations were shouted over the swelling noise. The smell of new wood and fresh paint, combined with the aroma of coffee and baked goods emanating from long tables along one wall, added to the atmosphere of conviviality.

Brad and I were greeted by Pastor Joe, his face beaming as he clasped our hands in his. "Welcome, welcome!" he said. He mopped his forehead with his handkerchief and stuffed it into his pocket. "I've been busy here all day and now so much excitement this evening…"

"Sit down for a bit, Pastor," said Sandy Wilcox, the church's youth director. "I'll greet people at the door."

"Well…"

"There are some chairs across the room," I said.

The three of us made our way over to the other side of the room, Pastor Joe waving to various people in attendance: the rabbi and a few members of the synagogue in Walnut Creek, Father Michael from St. Francis Catholic Church, and dozens of area business owners. He nodded a greeting in the direction of a group of parishioners, as two teen-aged boys racked the balls at the pool table nearby. "Some of my ecumenical colleagues are a bit shocked that we included a pool table in the hall."

"Like *The Music Man*—'Trouble starts with a T that rhymes with P that stands for Pool.'"

"You got it. But the idea is to get kids in here and give them space to gather. It's certainly not a pool hall. No smoking, drinking, foul language, or gambling—or out they go! Sandy Wilcox and her team do a good job of keeping order."

"I think it's a super idea," said Brad.

"Are your parents coming tonight, Meg?" asked Pastor Joe.

"I'm afraid not. Mom was hoping to get here, but she hated to leave Dad." Seeing the concern on the pastor's face, I added, "He's much better, but he still tires easily."

"Well, say hi for me and tell them they're both in my prayers."

"Thanks, Pastor. I'll do that."

Some people came up to chat with Pastor Joe. Brad and I gave them our chairs and headed for the refreshment tables.

"Oh, my favorite!" I said. "Green Jell-O."

Brad looked askance at me. "You're kidding."

Two men behind me echoed his remark. I turned. "Hey, Louis and Jon! Playing hooky from the restaurant tonight?"

"We decided to close early and come on over here," said Jon.

"We figured all our customers would be here, so…" said Louis. "But, Meg, green Jell-O? Really?"

"Really. Lime is my favorite. Mom used to serve Jell-O a lot. Unfortunately, she often put healthy things in it, like shredded carrots."

"I can't say I'm a fan of it," said Brad to me. "but I'm surprised you don't make it since you like it so much."

"Just got out of the habit, I guess." No way would I tell them that my attempts often ended in gelatin molds filled with watery or rubbery globs.

Nina and Ben Fulton came up behind us. "Be sure to grab a couple of those cookies at the end, there," said Ben, "the ones with the pink frosting. Nina made them."

"Better be quick," said Nina, "before Ben grabs them all."

"These cupcakes also look marvelous," said Celeste, as she joined us at the table. She, like my friend Sally Montrose, had a flair for looking wonderful in whatever she wore. Tonight, Celeste wore a mocha pencil skirt with a matching fitted jacket over a hot pink watered-silk blouse.

"That's a lovely suit," I said.

"Thanks, Meg," Celeste replied. "You're looking nice this evening."

"Thank you." I had on my little black dress, the staple of my non-sweatshirt wardrobe, but still felt a bit underdressed.

Brad whispered in my ear, "You're the best-looking woman here, Meg." I perked up just as Arch Donegal, who was in line just behind Celeste, added two of the cupcakes to a plate already heaped with homemade goodies.

Some of the Fultons' friends sitting a few feet away waved to them and indicated they were saving a couple of chairs for them. "Enjoy the evening," said Nina.

"Absolutely," said Celeste. The four of us walked away from the table and stood balancing our plates and paper cups of punch in a corner of the room near the windows.

"So how's our new community center coming, Arch?" Brad asked.

"Pretty good on the inside. We need some decent weather so we can work outside more."

"Any plans for the rest of the property?" I asked.

"Well, the old mortuary and crematory buildings are an eyesore, not to mention an ongoing reminder of their previous functions," Arch said. "The funeral home in Walnut Creek bought a few of the, er, appliances, and Jake Tigran's sold the leftover copper pipes, so it's a matter of tearing down the structures." He chuckled. "I made it sound easier than it is, but when the Winters boys have some time, we should be able to get those buildings out of there. Just need some cheap muscle."

"That would be—" My comment was interrupted by the sound of angry voices coming from outside the church. The windows were open a few inches to bring in some fresh air, and we could hear two people arguing.

"I know nothing about it. I'm as horrified as you are!" said Frieda Koenig.

"Yeah, sure," said Wallace Arnhart. "You can't win this election, Mrs. Koenig. Certainly not by employing those tactics." He held up a crumpled poster. It appeared to be the same one I gave him. "If this is how you're beginning your campaign, you'd better know I can produce as many posters and leaflets as fast as you can scribble on them."

"Mr. Arnhart, the very idea that I would stoop to ruining your posters…" Frieda spluttered.

"Wait until our debate, Mrs. Koenig. We'll see who's the best man—and the *only* man—for the mayor's position!"

Frieda stomped through the side door, her face incandescent with rage. Arnhart didn't follow her in, thank goodness. I would hate to see the argument continue inside and mar the celebration. Fortunately, the others in the room either hadn't heard the argument or had chosen to ignore it.

Bramble High School's glee club performed several songs with choreography, including Cher's "Believe," which had been topping the charts. A girls' foursome sang a couple of songs and told the audience that they were a barbershop quartet, and were going to be in a contest next summer. The group's choice of sing-along songs surprised us—they actually did include the old chestnuts, "Bicycle Built for Two" and "Let Me Call You Sweetheart"—the latter, a fun version involving dropping pronouns.

Marlene and Jake Tigran came up to us toward the end of the evening. "Great party!" said Marlene. "I had no idea girls sang barbershop music and could hit such low notes."

"I loved hearing them," I said. I looked around. "I don't know half the people here."

"Me neither, said Jake.

"How's the Bramble real-estate business going, Marlene?" asked Brad.

"It's slow, mortgage rates being more than eight percent. At least they're are down from where they were a few years ago." Marlene took a sip of the drink she was holding. "And thank goodness we don't have to contend with any more murders."

Chapter 10

March 1999

I usually snapped off the television right after the morning news was read. Not reported. Read. World events had not been truly reported on television since the golden era of Edward R. Murrow, Huntley and Brinkley, and Walter Cronkite. Today, I wasn't quick enough and glimpsed the beginning of an inane game show, hosted by a man trying to look younger with what my mother called "plastered surgery," and whose head was home to a jet-black hair piece. If it was made from an animal hide, it was a species known but to God.

A few minutes later, Harry Josten telephoned. "Meg, first, thanks for sending several Miss Polly columns. Always good to have a few in the hopper just in case. Also, I looked over the material you sent me, and I think the Bramble election would be an interesting piece for our readers. The whole men versus women thing, 'anything you can do I can do better,' and so forth." He chuckled. "No murders yet, I take it."

"Very funny," I answered. "I was beginning to think Bramble was the Midwest's answer to Cabot

Cove. And before you ask: yes, I like to watch *Murder, She Wrote.* And that's enough murder for me, thank you."

***

The snowdrops around the trees in my yard finally dared to show their heads; and jonquils, their yellow flowers atop brave green stalks, peeked out in hesitation as the sun's irresolute appearances hinted at spring's approach. Early spring weather could be mischievous, so I dressed warmly as I made my way to a meeting of the Millennium Arts Committee. The progress on converting the Victorian mansion to the Bramble Community Center was more and more visible. Arch Donegal and his crew were performing miracles, readying it for the multiple inspections needed before being approved for public use, and of course, for its grand opening during Bramble Heritage Week. Each day, more and more passers-by paused to admire the work.

I climbed the stairs to the Village Hall conference room and the hum of conversation greeted me as the MAC members helped themselves to coffee and sweet rolls. Knowing Frieda Koenig's penchant for thrift, I was certain that Sally provided the treats herself. I carried a donut and a cup of coffee to my place at the table as Sally tapped her water glass for order. As everyone nodded acceptance of Millie's minutes from the last meeting, the door opened and in minced a dapper little man dressed in a plum-colored suit, a pink shirt with a purple polka-dotted cravat at the neck, and a yellow vest with a gold chain heavy enough to weigh an anchor strung across his middle. A fob with an intricate design hung from the chain.

"I'm sorry, but I think you may be in the wrong room," Sally began.

"Oh, I doubt that," said the man in a British accent. "I'm Cyril Atkins and I'm here about the Arts Festival."

"Welcome, Mr. Atkins," said Sally. "We haven't begun our agenda, so if you'd like to tell us what's on your mind, this would be a good time."

Atkins walked to the other end of the table and stood for a moment facing the group. He twirled his mustache, its style decidedly un-English, more Salvador Dali than David Niven.

"My work is fine art," he began. "Not items constructed from left-over fabrics, rusted nails, and drinking straws. I am appalled to be assigned a stall in what you call the crafts area and insist that you reassign my work a location in accordance with its place in the world of *beaux arts.*"

No one moved. Celeste Farnsworth stood up and reached for a paper on the table and perused it. "Mister Atkins, I am the chair of the juried art committee and your name isn't on my list of accepted artists." She turned to Gladys Koenig. "Is he among your crafters, Gladys?"

Gladys said, "Yes, he is." Turning to Atkins, she said, "Anyone who doesn't submit their work via the juried art procedure is assigned a place with the crafts and needn't submit a copy of their art." She looked puzzled. "I see you described your work as 'miniatures.' Just what *is* that?"

I could almost see puffs of steam coming from Cyril Atkins' ears. "Madam, I am the foremost designer of miniature houses in all of Great Britain!" He placed several brochures on the table for us.

"Oh," said Gladys, her face clearing as she skimmed one of the publications. "Doll houses."

Atkins fumed. His mustache twitched furiously. His voice crackled with anger. "No! Miniatures—not children's toys!" The twitching picked up speed as he waved a brochure at the group. "As you can see from this, I am touring your Midwest with some of my best work. I included your town after Door County and Saugatuck because of Bramble's history as an art colony. I thought art would still be appreciated even after all this time. Perhaps I was mistaken." He started to reach for the extra brochures. "Perhaps I should withdraw!"

Before the further battle lines could be drawn, Sally interjected. "Perhaps, Mr. Atkins, Gladys, and Celeste could discuss this situation together with you? There's an empty meeting room down the hall."

The three marched out.

***

As Brad and I entered The Heron that evening, Barbara Wilcox greeted us and led us to our table where Sally was already seated.

"Thanks, Barbara. My husband should be here shortly," Sally said to the hostess handing around menus. "Barbara, we saw your sister at the church party. Sandy's doing a bang-up job as their youth director."

"She's definitely found her niche," Barbara replied. "I have too. I love working here."

As Barbara turned and walked back to the front of the restaurant, I said to the others, "Barbara—she used to be called Babsy—started as a shampoo girl at Gloria's. Bramble really looks after their own. Especially Gloria." I told the others about the financial career assistance she was giving Charlene Pullen.

Craig came up to the table, shook hands with Brad, kissed Sally, and asked her how the MAC meeting went.

"Another fun-filled meeting," Sally said. She pulled one of Atkins' brochures from her purse and passed it around the table as she recounted the episode between Gladys Koenig and Cyril Atkins. "After today's meeting, perhaps I should resign and let Madam Co-Chair here take over."

I was horrified.

Sally winked at me. "Never fear, Meg. Not that you wouldn't be good at taking over this job, but I'm stubborn. I refuse to let the turkeys get to me."

"Gobble, gobble," I replied.

"I'm not sure what you were talking about, but I hope you won't gobble our food tonight." Louis Briggs stood at our table with the wine list.

"Louis, good to see you." Brad said. "We promise. No gobbling. Savoring. The food here is a treat."

"That's good to know," Louis replied with a smile. "Otherwise, the chef would not be pleased. And I gotta live with the guy."

"It was great to see you and Jon at the Lutheran Church celebration," I said.

"Quite an evening. So many people turned out. The pastor was pleased," agreed Sally.

"It was fabulous," said Louis. "and those church ladies sure know how to bake!" He took our wine order. "Let me know if you need anything else," he said and headed toward the kitchen.

After dinner, we leaned back in our chairs. Our left-overs were boxed up to take home, but we were reluctant to end the evening just yet, so we ordered cappuccinos. "We've gotta stop meeting like this," I said. "I feel like I put on ten pounds after each meal."

It was nearly closing time and most of the tables were empty. As we sipped our drinks, we heard raised voices coming from another table. Sally glanced in the direction of the conversation, leaned toward us, and said in a sotto voice, "It's Arch and Celeste. I guess we didn't notice them come in."

We glanced in their direction. Celeste's face was flushed, her eyes narrowed with anger.

"You can't do this to me!" said Celeste.

Arch shrugged. "Sorry, Celeste. It's gone."

Celeste's voice rose, attracting the attention of the restaurant's remaining patrons. "Damn it, I won't put up with this, Arch! I won't!"

"Calm down, Celeste," Arch said.

Sally and I exchanged a glance. What woman ever calmed down when a man told her to do so?

"I *am* calm—calm enough to know what to do! You'll regret this!" Celeste banged the table with her fist, causing their silverware to jump and their coffee cups to rattle in their saucers. "Damn it, Arch, you've taken—" She stopped when she saw Louis striding from the kitchen toward their table. She gave him a shame-faced look. "We're going, Louis. Sorry for the fuss," she said. Arch tossed some bills on the table and the two hurried out.

Lights in The Heron dimmed, signaling imminent closure for the evening, and the four of us gathered up our things and left. We talked outside for a few minutes but didn't come to any conclusion about what we'd overheard. Celeste and Arch were a steady couple and we surmised they might marry sometime in the future. We concluded it was no more than a lover's spat.

Chapter 11

Early the next morning, before I visited my father at the rehab center, I stopped at the Bramble Police Station, which is housed in an old frame house. Other than the Midwest farmhouse exterior and walnut millwork inside, few portions remained of the station's prior existence as a private home. A hallway led past the police desk and interview rooms to the offices in the back. The police lockup, consisting of two small cells, was in a brick structure added to the rear of the house years ago. A squad car was parked in the small paved area in front. I pulled my Celica in next to it and went inside to talk with Bramble's police chief, Billy Koenig, about security at the Arts Festival—one of the "other duties as assigned" to me as the MAC co-chair.

I walked past the police desk and down the corridor where Ella Chapin, the chief's receptionist, looked up from her computer. "He's free, Meg," she said, nodding in the direction of the Chief's office. Her hair, sprayed and teased enough to accommodate nests of several small animals, remained immobile.

Billy Koenig resembled his brother, Fred, to the extent they could be identical twins. Unkind souls might call them Tweedle Dum and Tweedle Dee, but their friendliness and enthusiasm for their respective jobs were unmatched. When he saw me in the doorway of his office, he got up from his desk and lumbered over. He gripped my hand in both of his meaty paws. "Meg! Always good to see you. Come in, come in."

He went back to his desk and I took a seat across from him. I tried to read the papers scattered on his desktop. Upside down, they appeared to be invoices and other business papers. I told myself I wasn't really snooping. Even as a child, I read everything in sight, starting with the ingredients listed on the back of the cereal box every morning. I probably could've recited Wheaties ingredients from memory.

"So, Meg, you said on the phone that you wanted to talk about the security at the Arts Festival. I gotta say I have no idea why my brother and Frieda think they need more than what Bramble's police can provide. After all, we've even solved murders." He puffed up his chest until I feared for his shirt buttons.

I recalled solutions to the murders in Bramble were due to something other than the shrewd detecting skills of Bramble's finest, but I nodded and said,

"There'll be a lot of people from out of town coming to the Bramble Heritage Week."

"Well, we'll be upping our patrols, of course. But Frieda is determined to add some private security people."

As I pulled from my purse a copy of Brad's security cost analysis to relay a question he had, Billy's telephone rang.

The police chief picked up the receiver and sat upright in his chair. "What? Where? Are you sure?" After a few more minutes of conversation, he hung up and said, "Meg, I gotta cut this short. That was Wallace Arnhart. His store's been broken into."

I grabbed my purse and headed out the door after him. Brad's cost analysis question could wait.

***

An ambulance pulled away as I turned onto Main Street. A squad car was angled to the curb outside the Bushel O'Bargains and Chief Koenig pulled in next to it. I parked my car a few doors down from the store and grabbed a pad of paper and a pencil from my glove compartment. As I approached the store, Sergeant George Cadotte was directing two other police officers who were attaching left-over yellow tape printed with "Building Site: Keep Out" across the front door of the shop. Frugality at work.

Billy lifted the tape and went inside.

"George! What's happened?" I asked. Cadotte was a tall, good-looking man, with angular features he owed to his Native American heritage.

"Hi, Meg. I was patrolling just down the street when Arnhart's call came in. Someone got in last night and did some mischief."

"Anyone hurt? I saw the ambulance."

"Arnhart was roughed up. Bruises. A black eye. The paramedics checked him over. He didn't want to go to the hospital. Hope he sees a doctor and gets some pain meds. He's going to be sore tomorrow."

"Did he recognize who it was?"

Cadotte referred to his notes, "A couple of guys, he said. Knocked on the back door and pushed their way in. Wore ski masks. Were after money, but Wally put up a fight." George looked at me. "Actually, a dumb thing to do. He's lucky they weren't armed. Always best and safest to let 'em have the money."

Sage came running up. "What's going on?"

"And you are…?" asked Cadotte.

"I'm Sage Fletcher. I work here."

"Oh, yes. I thought you looked familiar," said Cadotte. "Norton's Drug Store, right?"

"Yeah, I work there too. A few hours here and there."

"Someone beat up Mr. Arnhart last night," he said to her.

I felt the presence of someone behind me and turned to see Cyril Atkins. His attire was a bit more subdued today: a loden green suit, a paisley bow tie, and dark green vest with the gold chain and fob.

"Hello, Mr. Atkins," I said.

"Hello, Miss, er…"

"Meg Smyth."

"Oh, yes. You're on the Millennium Arts Committee." He stroked his mustache, twirling its pointed ends. He nodded in the direction of the policemen. "Just came by for two or three bottles of wine. Didn't know there would be a bit of excitement as well."

After a few minutes, Sergeant Cadotte came over, the chief right behind him. "It's okay for you to enter," Cadotte said to us.

Billy added, "Yes, the place was dusted for prints. Wally needs to take inventory and give us a list of what's missing or damaged."

Arnhart came to the door. He had a bandage wrapped around one hand, and his right eye was nearly swollen closed. "Sage, go to the storeroom and clean up the mess!" he ordered. Not even a "please," I noticed. He continued to talk with Billy Koenig. "This has got to stop! I'm fed up being the victim of the crazies in this town! Posters I've paid good money for ruined. And now this!"

"You said there was only the one poster scribbled on—the one in front of your store..." began Billy.

"That's not the point. It's the principle of the thing."

Atkins and I slipped in behind Sage and walked with her to the back of the store. "Mr. Arnhart is certainly in high dudgeon," Cyril remarked.

"He certainly is," I replied. "Not a pleasant man in any event, but he does have a point. Looks like someone might be targeting him."

We reached the back of the store and surveyed the damage. Wine bottles from the shelves were smashed, leaving large, blood-colored splotches and puddles on the tile floor. Other items from nearby shelves—party supplies, paper goods, and the like—were scattered on the floor.

"Wow, Sage," I said. "You've got some work ahead of you." I noticed a mop, broom, and a couple of pails in the corner. "Let me help you."

Surprisingly, Atkins said, "I, too, shall assist forthwith." He fingered the fob on his watch chain. "I am a Master of Wine. If there are other bottles available to replace the broken ones, I can place new ones on the shelves." He picked his way across the floor and studied the bottles remaining on the shelves. "There are some very choice vintages here. Unusual."

I glanced at Arnhart, who had come up to us and was nodding in agreement and preening. Not many Masters of Wine crossed the threshold of Bushel O'Bargains.

"There are cases of wine in the back room," said Sage, indicating a door to her right. Cyril headed in that direction.

Sage and I wielded our tools and managed to get the debris cleared away. The stains on the floor, however, would need professional cleaning to eradicate them completely. Cyril did his part, scrutinizing wine labels, carrying others in from the back room, and placing them on the shelves while Sage replaced price tags in the slots on the shelves. And Wallace Arnhart? He stood and watched us work. Not so much because he was injured. More like the lord of the manor surveying his fiefdom. And his serfs. He inspected Cyril's arrangement of the shelves and nodded curtly to the Englishman. Never a thank you.

Before I left, I examined the back door. There didn't seem to be any noticeable damage. We finished up and headed toward the store entrance. Her day's work hours concluded at Bushel O'Bargains, Sage had her coat and purse over her arm, and Cyril carried a couple of bottles, presumably the wine he intended to buy.

"Are you a resident of Bramble?" Wallace Arnhart asked Atkins.

"No. I am visiting from England."

"Oh. Too bad. Otherwise, I'd give you a discount on the wine." No point in thanking him for his help or lowering the price for someone who won't be voting in the Bramble mayoral election.

Cyril Atkins made no reply. He paid Arnhart with a credit card and left the store.

"Off to another job, Sage?" I asked.

"Just a couple of hours at Norton's. I get to eat lunch there."

"I'll walk with you and grab a bite to eat. You certainly get around."

"School's expensive, so I need to sock away as much money as I can. The Fultons let me have the little room and bath over the hardware store. I clean up their store and help out a bit with the customers instead of paying rent."

"How nice of them. One of the advantages of a small town," I said, thinking of Gloria helping Charlene, and now, Nina and Ben assisting Sage. "What brought you to Bramble?"

"Oh, my grandfather talked about it a lot. He was a painter—worked in oils—and was here one summer at the Bramble Art Colony before World War Two."

***

I was itchy with sweat from my labors at the Bushel O'Bargains, so I had Sage pack a sandwich for me at Norton's to take home, where I took a shower and changed my clothes. I wolfed down my sandwich while Minerva, dozing on the kitchen window sill, gave me a brief look with slitted green eyes and went back to sleep. I envied her. A nap was tempting, but I really needed and wanted to visit my Dad.

The Walnut Creek Wellness Center's large, blue-tinted silvered windows gleamed in the sunlight. I had to park some distance away, the parking spots close to the door filled by people bent on exercise who went inside to jog around the indoor track. Although the Center was relatively new, the air inside was already infused with the stale cafeteria food smell common to hospitals, retirement homes, and other care facilities. As I walked along the corridor, I was pleased to hear Dad's laughter as I approached his room.

He gave me a broad smile as I entered his room. "Hi, Meg!" he said, "I was just trying to tell all my troubles to this nurse." He pushed himself up on his pillows. He had lost a bit of weight and his hair seemed wispier than before. But the sparkle in his eyes hadn't faded.

The nurse shook her head and—rolled her eyes. A kindred spirit. "Hi, I'm Vera, and you must be the daughter this guy keeps talking about."

"Yep, must be me. I'm his only and favorite daughter." I pulled up one of the synthetic wood chairs.

"I was just asking Vera why staff wake up patients in the middle of the night to see how they're doing. Or to take blood." He shook his head. "Maybe they're vampires and need to get a bite" Dad paused to make sure we appreciated his play on words "before scooting back to their coffins before daylight. The one today came in at 4:30 in the morning, woke me up, and—believe it or not—apologized for being late. Perhaps I'll call her Vampira next time."

"Not a good idea, Mr. Smyth," said Vera. "She might drain you dry. Accidentally, of course."

We chatted for a while before Vera left on her rounds.

"So, Dad, how are you? Mom said you had a bit of a temperature."

"I'm fine. Temp's normal. Helen frets a lot. I'm serious about the sleep interruptions. There's Vampira's visits, which I sort of understand, but the patient across the hall never uses her call button. She thinks that calling for nurse means screaming, 'Nurse! Nurse!' until someone answers. I'll be glad to get back to the apartment."

"Well, you look good, Dad. How long are you going to be in the hospital wing?"

"I'm here in the hospital section for one more day, then back to the apartment. I'll be coming here as an out-patient for physical therapy. He sighed. "All this healthy food. Does it really help you to live longer or does your life just seem longer? Dinner last night should've been called the Quiche of Death. And the nurses seem to have an inordinate interest in my bowel movements."

I laughed. "I can see you're back to your old self. Mom always said she could always tell when I was getting over a sickness by how ornery I got," I said. "Where is she, by the way?"

"She's at the apartment, I think. Hope one of us got a good night's sleep."

Another nurse rapped on the door frame and bounced in, her starched bosom leading the way. "Hello. I'm Betty. And how are we today?"

"I can only tell you about myself," Dad answered. "You'll have to fill us in on your own state of health."

The nurse gave him a blank look, not catching Dad's reference to the third-person plural used by nurses, Queen Elizabeth, newspaper editors, and the fifth little pig (if you count its cry of "wee, wee, wee" all the way home). Dad lifted his eyebrows at me and crossed his eyes. I turned away and chortled softly.

I stepped outside the room while the nurse tended to Dad. No one was in the corridor as I walked down to an alcove where visitors could wait. I noticed a copy of *War and Peace* on a table. I've had long waits at doctors' offices, but *War and Peace?*

Seeing Nurse Betty bustle from Dad's room, I went back in and chatted with him for a while longer before I left to return home.

Chapter 12

April 1999

Before long, the upcoming debate between mayoral candidates Wallace "Wally" Arnhart and Frieda Koenig was Bramble's primary object of interest, gossip, arguments, and discussion—not necessarily in that order.

The two candidates readily agreed on Sally and Craig Montrose as moderators. Brad, as Frieda's campaign manager was frazzled. What should've been a simple decision—where to hold the debate—was fraught with controversy. Brad and I spent many evenings going over local maps and generating ideas. "It's ridiculous," I said more than once. "Can't use the town hall because Frieda is the town's attorney and it would be prejudicial."

"And can't rope off Main Street for an hour or two, because the platform can't be too close to Bushel O'Bargains," commented Brad.

"Or have Norton's Drug and Sundries in the background, because some of Phil Norton's sundries—candy bars and breath mints, for heaven's sake—are in competition with the snacks carried by Bushel O'Bargains."

"And definitely not near the building site, since that's a major bone of contention in the race."

"Forget having Gloria's Glamour in the background, as it would be too 'woman-y,'" I said. "Same for Clipper Snip, which would emphasize men's interests—not to mention tossing Gloria, Frieda's image consultant, into throes of professional outrage, feeling as she does about the superiority of beauticians over barbers."

"Pastor Joe offered the new youth center, but someone brought up separation of church and state."

"Looks like we're down to the city dump or the cemetery," I said.

In the end, the debate was held at a grubby piece of property almost devoid of grass in back of the Sleepytime Motel—referred to as "The Royal Roach" by villagers—near the Interstate. Kids from the high school were recruited to clean up beer cans, broken glass, evidences of love trysts, and the like. Ben Fulton donated paint to spruce up the benches. Arch Donegal and some of his crew built the debate platform, over which Phil Norton hung red, white, and blue bunting.

Risking the wrath of strict interpreters of the Constitution, the Bramble Lutheran Church supplied folding chairs and tables stenciled with the church's name. Providing haute cuisine—or, perhaps, the *coup de grâce*—from his Liberty Café, Max Trent set up a booth to sell his Belly Buster Burgers and soft drinks at inflated prices.

***

A brilliant sun in a cloudless azure sky greeted Brambletonians as they began to assemble for the debate. Many brought their own lawn chairs, undoubtedly more for comfort than as a statement against the folding chairs as symbols of the Lutheran Church Rampant. Many women wore Frieda campaign buttons. Children scampered through the weeds, played in dust, spilled lemonade on themselves and others, and as things turned out, may have had the best time of all. Or, at least a better time than the two candidates.

A hush didn't exactly fall over the crowd, but it came close as the anti-feminist candidate, Wallace Arnhart, arrived in his BMW. He wore a white suit with a red and blue string tie and gave the crowd a vulpine smile as he strode confidently toward the platform. He looked around, possibly for a baby or two to kiss, but none were proffered. A toddler, her mouth ringed with chocolate ice cream, tightened her hand around the dirt she was clutching and wobbled toward him, her chubby legs churning. She grabbed his sleeve, looked up at him with a toothless smile, and burbled, "Chikkin Man! Chikkin Man!"

Forcing a smile which looked more like a snarling animal, Wally tried to pry the little girl's fingers away from his immaculate jacket, but she held it in a death grip. He pried. She howled. Tears ran down her little cheeks in dirty streaks. Her mother caught up with her, gently removed her daughter's hands from Wally's jacket, glared at him, and shouted, "You didn't need to be so rough. She thought you were Colonel Sanders!"

The crowd shrieked with laughter and chanted, "Chikkin Man! Chikkin Man!" Undaunted, or not daunted noticeably, Wally mounted the steps to the platform and, as politicians have done from time's beginning, stood waving and pointing to fans in the audience—to phantom friends, I always thought. No one waved back, although one man clucked and flapped his arms. Arnhart sat down on one of the folding chairs and wiped ineffectually at his dirty and sticky coat sleeve.

The minutes passed. The crowd grew restless. The townsfolk wanted to view, at last, what changes Gloria Morelli, Frieda's image consultant, had wrought upon the candidate. Having discovered chanting as an unexpected source of fun, the crowd began to roar in full voice, "Frieda! Frieda! We Wanna See Ya!"

At last, we heard repeated honking from the car bearing Frieda Koenig to the debate. Its tires throwing off billows of dust, a red Cadillac convertible, driven by her beleaguered campaign manager, moved regally through the grassless vacant lot. Placards bearing a photo of Frieda's face and her campaign slogan were attached to the car doors. In the passenger seat was Gloria, her fuchsia curls festooned with red, white, and blue ribbons.

Breathless, the crowd waited as Brad stopped the car, got out, and opened Frieda's door. The glitterati had arrived. Frieda's hair had been released from its usual bun and combed back in sausage-shaped waves. Cunning red star-shaped sequins twinkled in her hair. Lest the audience doubt her identity, Frieda wore a gabardine suit. As always, it fitted snuggly over a powerful, unyielding undergarment. But in a bold departure from tradition—no doubt originating with her image consultant—Frieda wore a new suit for this event: brilliant blue and sprinkled with red glitter, which shimmered in the sunlight and shed glitter with each step she took.

Her jaw clenched, a grim and determined Frieda stalked to the platform. She looked neither left or right. She sought no babies to kiss. She mounted the steps. She neither waved nor pointed. She tossed a tight-lipped smile in the direction of her opponent, who cast a look of hostile indifference back at her.

***

Sally and Craig Montrose stepped up to the microphone, introduced themselves, and went over the rules for the debate, including—an afterthought, I'm sure— a ban on cheering and chanting. Lots had been drawn beforehand, and Frieda spoke first. I sat a few rows back from the stage, and as the two candidates shook hands, I heard Arnhart mumble, "She won't know what hit her when I get through with her."

In her introductory remarks, Frieda Koenig cited her accomplishments and underscored her *pro bono* service to the village as its attorney. She was armed with an endless number of flip charts and a pointer. When Sally called, "Time!" she took her seat without protest. Craig moved the easel with the charts to one side.

Wally Arnhart began with a sententious speech, moralizing on the nepotism of the years of husband-wife rule of Bramble. He then waxed incredulous at the idea of using a prime Main Street location for the "artsy-fartsy" community center instead of a shopping center bringing in "real" revenue for businesses. Craig admonished Arnhart twice for exceeding the agreed-upon time limit.

As the afternoon wore on, Frieda droned on, flipping her charts while Wally tossed scalding jibes at them. Seeing the crowd's attention slough off and several people beginning to pack up their chairs, blankets, and children, Craig and Sally stepped up and thanked the candidates. The audience clapped as much for the candidates as for the end of a long afternoon. Both candidates gave a terse nod and walked to their cars without fanfare. Or chants. As I reached my car, I glanced over at Max's food tent. Judging by the overflowing trash cans filled with paper plates, cups, napkins, and bits of food, he had a successful day. Teens from the church began arriving to clean things up and load the folding chairs into the Bramble Lutheran van. "Thanks, kids!" I yelled. They grinned and waved at me.

Jon and Louis came up to me as I was getting into my car. "Hey, Meg," said Jon, "why don't you and Brad come by the house for a drink and a debrief about the day?"

"That sounds great," I said. "Brad has to get Gloria and Frieda back to their homes, and then return the Cadillac to Bert Schmidt's Rent-a-Car first. I'll pop on home, feed Minerva, and leave a note for Brad to join us."

***

As I opened a can of Minerva's food, she jumped up on the counter and sandpapered my arm with her tongue. Cat lovers would see nothing wrong with her being on the kitchen counter. I did have a few friends who would be appalled, but as long as they didn't pick cat hair from their teeth, they remained blissfully unaware of Minerva's fondness for counters and tables. I do keep guests out of my kitchen; it's best on so many levels. In my defense, most of the time, I wash down the counters before I put people food on them.

I took a quick shower, ran a comb through my hair, left the note for Brad, and walked next door to

Louis's and Jon's house. They had combined two adjoining cottages into arguably the nicest home in Cottage Row. Window walls took advantage of views of the lake and the professional landscaping wasn't overdone. Although much larger than the other cottages, their house blended in well with the smaller homes. Louis and Jon, with their usual charm—and delicious food, of course—often opened their home to their neighbors.

A faint moon was nudging the sun into retiring for the day, accompanied by the throbbing voices of frogs and the chirping of crickets. Here and there, fireflies flashed their presence. I hugged myself, thinking again how blessed I was to live in this place and at this time.

"We're over here," called Louis Briggs as I approached. "It's such a nice evening. We decided to use the deck."

Bug-repellent lamps—not those horrid ones that sound a game-show-like buzzer with each insect zapped—kept away the usual bevy of mosquitos and also cast a soft glow on the large deck and the riot of colorful flowers filling several large pots. Louis was at the deck's built-in bar. He was several years younger than his partner, Jon Dreher, who stood next to him, his arm casually over Louis's shoulder. Jon wore jeans and a T-shirt that clung to his muscular body.

"What'll you have, Meg?" asked Louis. "Jon made a chocolate gâteau with layers of chocolate whipped cream and strawberry and apricot preserves. Chocolate frosting, of course."

I gave silent thanks that I'd not succumbed to a Belly Buster at the debate. "Ooh, I've had that dessert at The Heron. It's wonderful. I can hardly wait." I thought for a moment. "Do you have coffee?"

"Of course," said Louis. "Coffee or perhaps, an espresso drink? Latte? Cappuccino?"

"A cappuccino sounds good, if it's not too much trouble."

"No trouble at all," Jon said. "We have a small espresso machine out here in the cabinet." He squeezed Louis's shoulder. "Louis will take good care of you."

I looked around. "Not that I miss it, but where's your Green Bay Packers patio umbrella?"

"The mice got it," said Jon. "We store our outdoor things in the shed out here, and evidently…"

"…they mistook the yellow stripes for cheese?"

The two men laughed.

"What a shame," I said with mock sincerity. I raised my cup of cappuccino in salute. "Go Bears!"

"That's my girl," Brad said as he came up to us and gave me a hug and shook hands with the couple. "What a day!"

"We must debrief and decompress," said Louis, "but first, what would you like to drink? Jon's made dessert."

"A giant beer," said Brad. He glanced at my espresso drink. "And maybe one of those a bit later."

After everyone was comfortably seated, Jon asked, "Brad, as Frieda Koenig's campaign manager, you were more involved in the debate than the rest of us, what's your take on it?"

"It was a debacle, to say the least," Brad said. "but wonderful entertainment."

"Okay," said Louis, "I have to say it." He was holding back laughter and could hardly speak. "When I saw Frieda emerge from the car, she…she looked like George Washington!"

"In drag," added Jon.

We laughed so hard we put our drinks down before we spilled them.

"That poor woman," I said, "Gloria did a number on her, although it could've been worse, I suppose. To me, the best-looking one of the bunch was the Secret Service guy."

The three men gave me blank looks.

"Brad," I said. "His dark suit, his dark tie, his shades. All he needed was an earpiece with a wire looped behind his ear."

"Too bad he had to be Frieda's driver." said Jon. "He could've run alongside the car. Added a professional touch."

"Oh, yeah," Brad responded. "My FBI colleagues would never let me live it down when I collapsed from exhaustion."

"Let's not forget Chikkin Man!" said Louis. "That alone was worth the whole day of speeches and charts. Colonel Sanders versus George Washington."

"That little girl will never eat anything from KFC again," Jon said.

We shared tidbits of the event until we were all holding our sides and gasping for breath from laughing and snorting.

"So…aside from that, Mrs. Lincoln, how was the play?" I asked. "What did you all think of the debate itself? Did either candidate win?"

"Trying to keep Wallace Arnhart in check was a task," said Jon. "Both Sally and Craig did what they could, but…"

Brad said, "It really wasn't much of a debate. Frieda about bored her audience to death with all those posters and graphs. I advised her against using so many, as it would give Arnhart more areas to attack—which, of course, he did rather than talking about what he planned to do as mayor. So much like politicians at all levels who attack their opponents and never tell the voters what their own platforms are."

Jon said, "Charts, nepotism, and her appearance aside, she really has been good at her job. She has my vote."

We all nodded.

"I don't think Arnhart won any points with the upscale folks with his 'artsy-fartsy' remark,'" said Louis, "and his encounter with that little girl turned off most of the women, I imagine. And a lot of the men, too, for that matter."

"I didn't see anyone throwing away their Frieda campaign buttons," added Jon. "Brad, is there another debate scheduled?"

"No! Another debate? You've got to be kidding! No! Absolutely not!"

"Gee, Brad, how do you really feel about it?" asked Louis. And we all laughed once more.

Jon went inside and emerged with the chocolate gâteau. It was magnificent. We ate in the reverent silence it deserved.

***

Brad and I walked slowly back to my cottage. "That dessert!" said Brad. "It must've been about six feet high. I'm stuffed." He eyed the plastic container I carried. "I hope you include me in your plans for demolishing that left-over."

"We'll see," I said, making no commitment to share. We walked a few steps more. "I really love those two. They're so comfortable with their sexuality that everyone else feels comfortable too. They've had encounters, that's for sure—probably more than we know, or want to know, about—but I think, Bramble has pretty much accepted them for what they are and what they add to our community. With so little love in the world, why do some people begrudge another a chance at happiness?"

"Speaking of love and happiness," said Brad. He turned me toward him and kissed me with increasing urgency.

We picked up the pace toward my house.

Chapter 13

Next morning

The aroma of fresh coffee wafted through my bedroom. Brad must already be up and downstairs. I glanced into the mirror as I performed an abbreviated version of my morning ablutions and combed my hair with my fingers. I would never be wasp-waisted, but unless I watched my weight, I'd soon need to wear loose tops with dolman sleeves to accommodate dolman arms. I thought of the chocolate gâteau in the refrigerator. Scarlett O'Hara's famous line came to mind: "Tomorrow is another day." For additional support in my dietary procrastination, I recalled Miss Scarlett also said, "As God is my witness, I'll never be hungry again." Not that I was in any danger.

I opened the closet and looked over my limited wardrobe. I had more black turtlenecks than Steve Jobs. From the bed, Minerva made little cries of cat ecstasy as she rolled in the still-warm sheets. I left her squirming in feline delight and went downstairs to the kitchen. "Hi, sleepyhead," greeted Brad. He poured me a cup of coffee and kissed the top of my head.

"Hi yourself," I replied. There were some dirty

dishes in the sink. "What did you have for breakfast?"

He had the grace to look guilty. "Um…"

"Tell me you didn't eat all the dessert left over from last night."

"I didn't eat all the dessert left over from last night," he repeated in rote.

I opened the refrigerator. He hadn't lied. There were two smallish bites left. The fates must've heard my alarm over my rising weight.

He gave me the goofy, lopsided grin I loved.

I sighed and took out the remains of the gâteau, grabbed a fork from the drawer, and brought the coffee and the morsels of dessert over to the table. I plunged my fork into what remained of the dessert.

"What are your plans for today?" I asked as I brought my dishes over to the sink.

"I'm thinking of doing some odd jobs around my house," he said. "And a bit of office work. I'm trying to do more business stuff at home and not go into the Loop as much. As you know, I'd really like to take early retirement. I have enough years in, and I'd really like to do something else, maybe something less bureaucratic."

"Like eating dessert for breakfast? Or becoming a professional campaign manager?"

He chuckled. "I don't want another career, exactly, but I need to do something. I don't want to sit on my porch and watch the world go by."

"You'll wait a long time to see the world go by in Bramble," I said lightly. But my stomach plummeted. *What does he see as our future? Is there an* our future? *For that matter, what do* I *want?*

***

After Brad left to attack his unending list of things to do at his cottage, I turned on my laptop and began an email to Harry Josten about yesterday's debate. Putting thoughts aside about what the future might hold for Brad and me was difficult, but the act of writing about the Arnhart–Koenig debate soon pushed errant thoughts from my head as I lost myself in the language of words. My reporter days at *The Journal-Times* office stood me in good stead. The newsroom desks were butted together, and I soon learned to shut out the clatter of typewriters and the cacophony of several telephone conversations taking place at the same time.

Lost in creating deathless prose, I jumped when I heard an argument coming from next door. My kitchen window was open, but I didn't want to be a nosy neighbor—even though I was planning to be just that—so I stood to one side of the window and peeked around the curtain. Cam had a small suitcase in his hand, and he and Willow were about to get into their car. Willow, her coat gapping open around her pregnant belly, clutched his arm.

Cam's mother, Irie, all but breathing fire, stood on their porch and screamed, "I am a midwife! I am revered and honored in Jamaica! Children I birthed call me 'Mama!' There is no need for hospital! No need for maternity ward! Willow, go back inside and I will take care of you! Your little girl should be born at home where I can be with you all the time and make sure you learn how to take care of my son's baby correctly. And you can rest while I give my Cameron good, home-cooked meals."

One didn't need to be the brightest star in the heavens to conclude it was time for the Podolski baby to be born, and the couple was headed to the hospital. And Irie was the tiniest bit unhappy about it.

"Mother, we've been through this a hundred times," said Cam. Even at a distance, I sensed the effort he was making to keep his voice steady. "Our baby is going to be born in the hospital where she and

Willow will have wonderful care. All the modern equipment. Obstetricians I know personally. Willow and I have attended several classes about caring for an infant." He paused. "And I like Willow's cooking!"

"Atta boy!" The three turned and looked toward my house. Uh-oh, they must've heard me. I didn't dare move or even breathe.

The break I provided in their exchange was enough for Cam to turn from the argument and assist his wife into the car. He came around to the driver's-side door and opened it. "Mother, please go on inside. We need to get moving."

Irie crossed her arms in front of her, raised her chin in defiance, and glared. Cam got in the car and backed the car out of the driveway, narrowly missing two massive clumps of native grasses. His mother remained rooted to her spot until the car had left the driveway. She raised her arms skyward, muttered something, then went inside, and slammed the door.

I sat down at the computer again and marveled at how much drama there could be in such a short time. The gala church event, a store break-in, an election debate, a family flap next door, and a baby on its way. Small-town life was exhausting.

***

I sat at my computer, connected to one of the AOL local phone numbers, and sent off my story to my editor, Harry Josten.

I was rummaging around in the refrigerator looking for items for lunch, when the phone rang. It was Harry.

"Wow, that was fast, Harry," I said. "I just sent you that e-mail."

"Yeah, Meg, sometimes we're the victims and sometimes we're the beneficiaries of technology, that's for sure," Harry said. The line was silent.

"Are you still there, Harry?" I asked.

"Yes, I am." I could hear him take a deep breath. "That's what I wanted to talk with you about." Another deep breath. "Meg, I've decided to retire at the end of this year. We've worked together for a long time, and I wanted you to be among the first to know."

I was stunned. "No! You can't mean it."

"Well, Meg, I've been thinking about it for a while now. I've been with *The Journal-Times* for nearly forty years. Started out as a copy boy, hustling news stories from desk to desk, reporters to editors, and back again. He sighed. "*Tempus fugit.* And not only does time fly, but time also changes things too, Meg. Too fast in both cases, if you ask me. Our publisher sent me a BlackBerry—some sort of new hand-held gizmo—and I have no idea how to use it. Or why I'd want to." He chuckled. "I'm a confirmed Luddite, I guess. In favor of trailing-edge technology. I agree with the late Mike Royko that the Internet is not an information highway but 'an electronic asylum filled with babbling loonies.'

"You've been back in the building from time to time, Meg, and you've seen how different things are now. Everything's getting computerized. Hot lead and linotype operators are a thing of the past. Desktop publishing is the new way of doing things, and every person who can type with two fingers considers himself a typesetter." Harry gave a disgusted snort. "I often wonder if newspapers even will be printed in the future."

"Oh, Harry…"

"Just ignore my gloom and doom soapbox, Meg. Anyway, I didn't want you to learn about my plans via the newsroom grapevine. And, of course, your Miss Polly column will continue on, syndication and all."

"When do…?"

"Oh, I'll be winding things down until the end of the year. They'll give me the traditional rubber chicken dinner—Pullet Surprise—and a plaque." He chuckled again. "The United Nations proclaimed 1999 as The International Year of Older Persons. I haven't a clue what that means, but whatever it is, I'm going to enjoy every moment of it before it's over!"

Chapter 14

May 1999

Work on the Bramble Community Center continued steadily and the building was almost ready for use. The number of Bramble residents gawking at the building site increased daily. Bramble was opinion rich. Every person had something to say about the construction. Even today, with a light mist falling, a dozen or so Bramble residents were bunched outside the temporary fencing. From across the street, where I'd parked my car, I saw that today, however, the crowd was silent, focused on something else going on behind the fence.

Arch Donegal, his mop of red hair matted from the rain, stood on an overturned wooden crate at the site. He took several gulps from the coffee cup he held and addressed the workmen. The men booed and shouted. A few of them shook their fists and swore at him. I tightened the hood of my windbreaker jacket and walked over to the site to find out what was going on. It didn't take me long to find out. The payroll was late.

Wallace Arnhart came up behind me and spoke in my ear. My skin crawled and I took a step away from him. His breath was worse than a caravansary. "See what I mean, Ms. Smyth?" he hissed. "I've heard that this isn't the first time the men have had to wait to be paid. This town needs a man to run it." A few people around us overheard him and nodded in agreement.

Arch raised his hands in an attempt to settle the workers. "I'm going over to talk with the mayor right now," he said. "We'll get this figured out." He finished the last of his coffee, then jumped down from the crate. Tossing the empty cup into a nearby trash basket, he walked over to his pickup truck. He drove off toward the village hall.

He never arrived.

Chapter 15

Later that day

I had a quick lunch at Norton's Drugs and started home. The rain had increased to torrents and storm clouds obscured the sun, giving the sky an odd greenish color. I saw the flashing lights of emergency vehicles even before I turned onto Red Fox Lane, so I parked in Brad's driveway rather than continuing on to my cottage. I got my umbrella from my trunk, grabbed my notebook and pencil, and walked over to where Chief Koenig and Sergeant George Cadotte were talking with the Seminole County Coroner, Jim Dowd. Dowd was a handsome man of about forty, his bearing self-assured and dignified even wearing a shapeless, oversized rain slicker and dark-green rubber waders. Nearby, two men were loading the coroner's van with a large black vinyl bag used for only one purpose.

Dowd squelched through the mud toward me. "Hi, Meg."

"What's happened, Jim?" I asked.

"A woman walking her dog along the shore saw the truck weave down the street and end up in the lake." She's over there. He gestured to a squad car where a woman, wrapped in a blanket, sat in the back seat. "She ran over and called the police, but she couldn't do anything for the driver."

He pointed to a wild tangle of brush and reeds at the shoreline. Branches of the willow trees along the shore trailed in the water. In the downpour, I hadn't noticed the crumpled vehicle, which was partially in the lake. I recognized the truck.

"Oh, Jim, is it…?"

"Yes, I'm afraid so. It's Arch Donegal."

***

I thought of Celeste. She needed to know about Arch. Billy Koenig would notify her, but someone should be with her. But who? Her sister, Gloria Morelli! When she first moved to Bramble, Celeste lived with her sister on Cottage Row. I never could see much resemblance between the two women, and was willing to bet that Celeste didn't have her hair done at Gloria's Glamour. And definitely not at the Clipper Snip. I didn't see Gloria Morelli in the small group gathered at the accident site, so I walked to her house, rang the bell, but no one was home.

Brad pulled into his driveway as I was getting into my car. He came over to me. "What's going on?"

"Oh, Brad, it's Arch. He's been in an accident. He's dead." Brad drew me to him and thumbed a tear from my cheek. "I saw him drive off from the Community Center work site earlier. I can't believe he's gone. Celeste probably doesn't know about Arch yet. Gloria isn't home. Celeste needs to have someone with her…"

"Get in my car, Meg. Celeste is in her office at the Wellness Center."

"How do you know?"

"She made an appointment with me for this afternoon. She was concerned about her finances. I was running errands and came home to pick up my laptop. He pushed back his coat sleeve and checked his watch. "I'll run inside and get my computer, although she probably won't be wanting to talk business right now."

"I'll come inside for a minute, Brad, and call Gloria's shop. See if Gloria's there."

Gloria's shop assistant answered. Gloria wasn't in that day.

Brad looked at me. "Do you think we should phone Celeste from inside about Arch? My car phone doesn't pick up signals when it rains."

"Would be better in person. Harder. But better."

***

The driving rain diminished to a light rain as we drove to Walnut Creek. Rivulets slid down the windshield as we pulled into the lot at the Wellness Center. We walked inside. Brad stabbed the elevator button, the doors swished open, and we rode up to the third floor. Across from the elevator was the door marked "Celeste W. Farnsworth, M.D."

Celeste was alone in her office and looked up as we approached. She dabbed her eyes with a tissue as she led us over to a conversation area at one end of her office. "Oh, Brad, I forgot our appointment. And Meg…" Her voice trailed off.

I began, "Celeste…"

"I know about Arch. Sergeant Cadotte was here a little while ago and told me what happened. I tried getting my sister, but…"

"I'm so sorry," Brad said. "What can we do to help you?"

"I-I really don't know. I feel so terrible." She picked at the balled-up tissue in her hand.

"Why don't we come home with you?" I said. "Get you settled this evening. You've had quite a shock. We can keep trying to get Gloria from there."

"That's so kind, but…"

"No buts about it," said Brad. "I'll take you in your car and Meg can follow in mine. That way, you'll have your car at home when you need it."

After a few more feeble protests, Celeste grabbed her brief case and purse, and took her jacket and an umbrella from the coat tree in the corner.

***

Celeste lived in a townhouse in Walnut Creek, a short distance from the Wellness Center. We left our wet shoes and coats in her front hallway and walked into the living room. The carpeting, sofa, and two wing chairs were white. Bookshelves on one wall provided most of the color in the room. It was so quiet, I could almost hear us breathe. Celeste went around and turned on two or three lamps, bathing the room in a soft glow.

"Celeste," I said, "I'll call Gloria again. Why don't you go get into something comfortable?"

"You don't need to ask me twice," she said, with a wan half-smile. "I think I'll take a shower. There are drinks in the refrigerator, glasses in the cabinet next to it. Help yourselves. I have some food…"

Brad interrupted. "No cooking tonight. How 'bout if I get some take-out food for us? Do you like Chinese? Burgers?"

"I'm not very hungry," she replied, "but Chinese sounds good. Maybe some egg drop soup. There's a menu in the drawer by the phone in the kitchen."

Celeste went upstairs to change and Brad headed for the kitchen. I sat on one end of the couch and looked around. Almost sterile. No knick-knacks or personal items. Just books. I walked over to the wall of bookshelves. All of Celeste's books related to her career—*Gottmann's Marriage Clinic, Alcoholics Anonymous, Physicians' Desk Reference,* and others.

I was about to return to my place on the couch when I spotted something wedged in the corner of one of the shelves. I moved three or four books, and found a framed photo, face-down. I turned it over: Celeste and Arch at some outing. The glass was cracked. I was looking at it more closely when I heard Celeste moving around upstairs. I placed the photo back where I had found it. Brad came into the living room as I was trying to put the books back the way they were.

"That kitchen. All white with a set of eighteen different kinds of knives made in Germany. Why would anyone need eighteen—what are you doing, Meg?"

I dropped the book I was holding. "Brad! You startled me. I was just, um…" I picked up the book as I struggled for a reason to give him as to why Celeste's books were in disarray.

"You're up to something, Meg. What?"

"I'll tell you later," I replied, tapping the spines of the books into line.

The doorbell rang just as Celeste reached the bottom of the stairs. Brad and I turned and gaped at her. I had no idea women, other than Loretta Young, wore peignoirs.

I recovered and opened the door. Gloria stood outside, a small suitcase in one hand and a large bag of food from The Heron in the other. She rushed in and hugged Celeste.

Brad still held the menu from the Chinese restaurant. He and I looked at each other, awkward now that help had arrived and Celeste wouldn't be alone tonight.

"Thank you so much, Brad, Meg," said Gloria as she released her sister. "I saw the last police car pull away from Cottage Row as I got home from doing some shopping. When I heard what had happened..."

"Um, Meg and I will be going, Celeste," said Brad, "now that you're in good hands." He put the menu on an end table. "And with good food."

"Thanks, Brad. Meg," Celeste said, touching our arms. "Brad, I'll call you. I still need to discuss my financial situation with you."

Chapter 16

Two days later

Arch Donegal's death continued to nag at me. The more I tried to wrap my thoughts around what was bothering me, the more it eluded me. Confused dreams plagued me each night, and this morning I awoke, unrested, with the bedclothes twisted around me. I needed to find out more details about the crash. I made an appointment to visit the coroner's office. I yawned as I brewed a pot of coffee, thinking of Arch and his fondness for it.

The Seminole County seat, the courthouse, and the coroner's office formed a triad of tired and weary buildings that were not aging gracefully. I pulled into the equally tired and weary parking lot. Bright green sprigs of weeds did their best to decorate the cracked pavement with marginal success. The Seminoles never lived anywhere near Walnut Creek and it was an ongoing mystery as to why they were given the dubious honor of having a Midwestern county named for them.

Stepping around several large potholes filled with rain water, I entered the coroner's office building and pushed open the reluctant revolving door. I walked over to the swarthy uniformed security guard seated at the small reception desk, who looked up as he was ending a phone call, "Okay, I'll see you at five to one." He quickly slid his hand over a document on his desk.

"Hi. Can I help you?" The name on his shirt below his company's logo read "Frank Makar."

"I'm here to see the coroner."

Makar stood up and slid the sign-in book across the counter to me.

I filled in my name and handed back the register.

Just then, the telephone rang. "Gotta get this," the guard said. "Do you know where the coroner's office is?"

"Yes. I've been here before. Thank you."

As he turned away from me to answer the phone, I glimpsed the corner of the paper he'd covered up, but I could see only five figures in the corner—8 AQUE—without moving the paper and attracting Frank Makar's attention.

I turned and walked down the hallway, its walls painted the same nasty shade of green—olive drab, the Army called it—used on tanks, barracks, and, until forty-odd years ago, mailboxes. My footsteps echoed on the floor, the asphalt tile yellowed by myriad coats of wax covering whatever the original color was.

The coroner's office suite was something else. I longed to kick off my shoes and wiggle my toes in the lush carpeting. Dominating the reception area was a large oil painting of Jim Dowd—salubrious, tanned, clear-eyed—rendered in a style reminiscent of portraits of Napoleon, but without one of Dowd's hands plunged inside his (Dowd's) jacket. The coroner's pert young receptionist looked up from filing her nails, shifted her chewing gum to her other cheek, and mumbled at me to enter the inner office.

Dowd, dressed in sharply creased khaki pants and a turquoise polo shirt, its shirt collar artfully turned up to look preppy and hip, rose from his desk chair. He smiled, his teeth like piano keys (the white ones). "I rather hoped you'd turn up, Meg. We share an interest in what the dead can tell us."

Before I could process that disturbing thought, Dowd extended his hand for me to shake. Other visitors to the morgue might recoil at the smell of formaldehyde or the sight of misshapen things floating in jars on the shelves, but I had grown up viewing with fascination the jars of fetuses at Chicago's Museum of

Science and Industry. No, for me, the worst part of visiting the morgue was shaking hands with Jim Dowd. Not only did I have difficulty suppressing thoughts of where the coroner's hands had been, but his grip was always moist and slimy, like a sponge left overnight in cold, greasy dishwater. To my credit, I didn't flinch, but as soon as I had a chance, I furtively wiped my hand on my jeans.

The grim hospitality ritual over, I asked him about Arch Donegal's accident. "Jim, it seems odd that he ended up in Prairie Lake. I saw him leave the work site to drive to the village hall. That's in the opposite direction from the lake."

Dowd opened a tan folder on his desk and removed a sheaf of paper bristling with arrow markers. He thumbed through the pages until he found the one he wanted and looked it over. "Well, Meg, it isn't surprising. I suspect he was disoriented and had no real idea where he was. Definitely shouldn't have been driving. Fortunately, he was alone and it was a one-car crash, so no one else was killed or injured."

"Disoriented?"

The coroner looked down at the file again, and traced a line on the paper with his finger. "The preliminary tox report showed he had a significant amount of morphine in his system. The accident happened because Mr. Donegal was operating a motor vehicle while under the influence of a powerful opioid, which may well have caused him confusion, drowsiness, or even trouble with breathing." Dowd looked up. "Meg, he would have survived the crash. The drug overdose is what killed him."

I was stunned. "I haven't known Arch for very long," I said, "but I've never seen him drink more than a beer or two—and certainly never thought of him using drugs. His only addiction was coffee. He must've consumed gallons of it each day."

"That's interesting, Meg. The morphine was found in his coffee."

***

The coroner's report left me twitchy, or what my Mom would call "at sixes and sevens"—her expression for being out of sync or bewildered by a situation. Which I certainly was. So odd that Celeste Farnsworth, with her extensive background in addiction counseling and treatment, hadn't picked up on Arch's drug habit. They'd been seeing each other for several months.

I had a chilling thought. Surely, he wouldn't have taken his own life in such a way—drugs at the work site? And driving off afterwards? Risking his own life and that of others?

That left two possibilities: accidental, unintended overdose in his coffee or—murder.

Chapter 17

A few days later

Cameron and Willow Podolski arrived home at the same time I was parking my car in my driveway. I waved to them and they motioned me over to see their new baby girl.

Willow held the baby, almost hidden in a fuzzy pink blanket. I admit that most new babies look pretty much the same to me: all wrinkly faces with eyes that seem oddly old as they view their new world. But the Podolski child, with her light caramel skin and dark eyes, was a heart-breaker. "She's so pretty. What's her name?"

"Tamila Chandice," Willow replied. "Tamila means 'dearest to the heart,' and Chandice is Jamaican for 'extremely smart and talented.'"

"How lovely…" I started to say, when One Who Spreads Harmony shrieked from the doorway. "Cameron! Willow! Come inside now with the baby. It's cold!" They hastened inside.

Turning to me, Irie Podolski shouted, "Thugs beating on that nice Mr. Arnhart! And then a murder! What do you know about these terrible things?"

I kept my voice level. "I'm sure the police will catch who's doing it."

"Pah! The police. Hmmph! Bramble not a nice place to live. I will talk to my son. We need to move from this dangerous place!"

Before I could reply, Irie turned on her heel and slammed inside.

I wasn't sure why she asked me what I knew, but I slunk off like a scolded dog. I didn't know much about either of the two crimes. I planned to talk with Billy Koenig soon about Arch's death and get an update on what happened at the Bushel O'Bargains.

My lack of sleep caught up with me, so after lunch, I stretched out on the couch for a few minutes. Minerva, all four legs tucked under her in her loaf-of-bread position, dozed from the ottoman. The few minutes turned into hours and I awoke as the golds and pinks of sunset seeped through the windows.

***

In that groggy-not-quite-refreshed stage that often follows a nap, I stretched and looked at the clock. Time to think about dinner. As I was deciding between an omelet or peanut butter on toast, Brad phoned and asked me over to his house for burgers on the grill. I changed clothes, checked my face for pad marks left from the couch cushions, and grabbed a bottle of wine from the pantry. Stars were beginning to poke through the darkening sky as I walked the path along the lake to his cottage.

Brad was fussing with the charcoal. Pronouncing the coals suitably gray, he placed the patties on the grill. "I see you brought something to quench our thirst," he said, as he gave me a hug. "We'll eat inside. It's getting chilly."

"I'll bring the wine in." I put the wine on the kitchen counter and walked through the downstairs. He hadn't been puttering around with minor tasks. All of the downstairs rooms were painted off-white, and it looked like a lot of work was ahead for him. The walls along the staircase were down to the studs.

"Brad," I said as I sat down in one of the lounge chairs outside, "you've done a lot of work on your house recently. I haven't been inside for a while. It looks great! The light-colored paint really makes the rooms seem so much larger and brighter."

"Yeah. The house needed some cheering up." He winked and added, "When you're not here, that is. I asked Jake Tigran's wife, Marlene, for some tips. Being in real-estate, she knows what things add to the resale value."

"Adding to the resale value of my house is the only reason my house has a kitchen."

Brad smiled and continued, "There was a lot more to do here than I thought." He gave a rueful shake of his head. "I guess that's pretty typical of re-modeling. I've tried to give as much business as I can to Ben Fulton. It's getting harder for his local hardware store to compete with the big-box supply stores like the one out by the Interstate."

"I love watching Ben add up sales on butcher paper with that flat wooden pencil, and send it with the payment up to the loft where Nina sits and runs the cash register."

"I bet he rarely makes a mistake in his math. No calculator for Ben, that's for sure!"

***

After dinner, Brad and I were sitting in his living room, talking about recent happenings in Bramble, when the doorbell rang.

Celeste Farnsworth was at the door. "Oh, Brad, I didn't know you had company," she said. She turned to go. "I'm so sorry. I didn't see any cars in your driveway, but of course, Meg would walk or…" She paused. "I just couldn't stand not knowing what to do. I kept going over and over things in my mind. And my sister Gloria staying with me, hovering, telling me over and over how 'concerned and worried' she is. I finally sent her home, and…" Celeste stream of words stopped and a sob escaped.

I tried not to stare. Gone was the confident professional in designer suits and Christian Louboutin shoes, every hair in place, makeup subtle, yet fastidious. Tonight, she looked more like a bedraggled waif. I could see why her sister was concerned.

"Please come in, Celeste," Brad said.

"Oh, but I don't want to interrupt anything."

"You're not, Celeste," I said. "I know you wanted to consult with Brad. I was leaving in a bit, anyway," I fibbed.

"No, no, please, Meg, stay. I don't mind if you hear what I've come to talk with Brad about. In fact, perhaps it would be best for you to stay, what with your experience with criminals and all."

I veered away from asking what my experience with criminals might mean to her. First Irie, now Celeste. What am I? The font of all knowledge of things criminal? "Would you like some coffee?" I asked.

The three of us moved to the small dining-room table. Celeste unzipped her Coach shoulder bag and pulled out some folders and documents. Brad took them and read through them, making notes on a yellow legal pad.

He put down the papers and asked, "What happened here, Celeste?"

"I trusted Arch Donegal. That's what happened," she replied, bitterness edging her voice. "We planned to marry and he needed someone to invest in the construction business he wanted to start in Bramble or Walnut Creek—in this area, anyway. So I took a good-sized distribution from my IRA."

Brad sifted through the papers and said gently, "You almost emptied the account, Celeste."

"I know, I know. I feel so stupid. And now my income tax will be so high, I can't possibly pay it." She took a tissue from her purse and wiped her eyes, blotching her cheeks with mascara.

"Celeste, we can put together a payment plan with the IRS. I can help you with that." Brad said as he wrote on the pad. "Um, with Arch, er, gone, do you know where he might have put the money you gave him? Bank? CDs? Stock market?"

"It's gone, Brad. Gone." She exhaled a shuddering breath. "All my training, all my years counseling addicts and their families. And I fell for it."

"Was he addicted to drugs?" I asked. This might be the answer to why Arch died the way he did.

"No. I would've noticed drug or alcohol addiction. My field is substance abuse. At least, I think I would've seen it. I don't know even that anymore." She took a deep breath. "No. Arch was addicted to gambling."

The three of us sat in silence for a few moments.

Celeste continued, "Please understand. I'm not making any excuses, but my colleagues and I each specialize in treating specific kinds of addictions. I've studied other forms of addictions, of course—food, sex, gambling—but I guess I wasn't attuned to it." She sighed. "I asked him for receipts for my tax purposes. He dodged me for a long while, gave me excuses. It all came to a head that night at The Heron. I'm sure you saw us arguing.

"One more poker hand, the next horse or football game, just another this or that, and he'd pay me back. The thing is," she continued, "he would never be able to pay me back. The kind of gambling he did—high-stakes, back-room—wasn't legal. He owed money to some very rough characters. He even found threatening, hand-lettered notes in his truck—something about being marked for death."

"Celeste, you need to go to the police station in the morning and make a formal statement about all this, particularly the illegal gambling," advised Brad. "I'll go with you if you like."

"I can't," she said, her voice quivering. "I'm a well-known expert in the field of addictions treatment." She paused. "It's really not a matter of pride—well, at least, not much. My patients, even ones I've treated in the past, might doubt the treatment and therapy they received from me. It doesn't take much for people who are shaky in their recovery to think of an excuse to go back out and take up where they left off."

Brad leaned forward in his chair. I've never seen him look so serious. "Celeste, as you know, I'm with the FBI and a federal law enforcement officer, so if you don't talk with the police, I'm obligated to do so."

"But—"

Brad was adamant. "No excuses, Celeste. I'll go with you tomorrow to the police station."

A tremulous sigh escaped her. "Okay, I'll go."

***

After she left, Brad walked me home. He declined to come in. "I'll pick you up early tomorrow, Meg, so we can get to the police station before Celeste arrives, and see what the situation is."

He noticed my surprise. "Meg, I knew you'd want to be there. You can take a reporter out of the newsroom, but—"

"You know me too well," I said, "even in the Biblical sense."

I thought about Celeste's predicament as I slipped on my L.L. Bean pajamas—no peignoirs for me. Celeste and Brad knew each other when they were neighbors on the East Coast. Brad and his wife had a baby who died of SIDS and their marriage couldn't withstand the emotional strain it caused, so Brad consulted Celeste, who became his therapist for a year or two, and helped him to deal with, and eventually, accept the loss of both his child and his marriage.

I admit to a twinge or two of jealousy once in a while, but I'm glad Brad is the kind of man who wants to help a friend—man or woman—who's stuck in a mud hole of pain and self-doubt.

But as I got ready for bed, I felt the blood in my neck pulsing. What did Brad mean about adding resale value to his house? I kid about my kitchen, but Brad was serious, had talked to Marlene. I almost asked what he meant, but I didn't want him to think I was assuming our relationship would last, or that we would share a home in the future. It wasn't a conversation I was ready for yet. To be truthful, I still wasn't sure what I wanted. But still…resale value?

Chapter 18

The next day

Brad and I entered the Bramble police station the next morning. Brad went over to the desk and spoke with the officer on duty. I sat on one of the hard plastic chairs lining the lobby. After a short conversation, Brad came over and sat down beside me and without preamble, said, "Celeste was brought in by the police last night. She's already in custody. The police came to her condo last night and took her to the station in a squad car."

"Oh, Brad, how awful. Not in handcuffs, I hope?"

"No. From what I gathered, Sergeant Cadotte was the officer in charge and spared her that. Even so, I'm sure the word is around town by now."

"You mean she's here? In a cell? Does Gloria know that Celeste is in custody?"

"Fortunately, Celeste hasn't been arrested yet, but she is being detained. She spent the night in the lockup. Celeste called her sister last night and told her we were coming in this morning and would be with her. Gloria needed to go to her salon to reschedule appointments and such, and will try to join us later.

"Oh, Brad. I can't imagine Celeste spending time in a jail cell. Does she have a lawyer?"

"Gloria hired an attorney from a Walnut Creek criminal law firm, Chatsworth, Chatsworth, and Plunk. One of the partners, Danford T. Chatsworth, should be arriving any time now."

From my background at *The Journal-Times,* I knew a bit about the subject of police custody. "I'm not sure, but I think she must be charged and brought before a judge within forty-eight hours or released. Brad, do you think she's going to spend more time in jail?"

"If the prosecutor files charges against her, yes. She'll be transported by the police to Walnut Creek tomorrow or the next day to appear before the magistrate at the Seminole County courthouse. If she's charged with murder, she'll be moved into the county jail right away. Bail would then be a problem."

"Surely, you don't think they'll charge her with murder?"

"I don't know, Meg. I really don't know."

Time dragged by. Where was that lawyer? These chairs should be added to the list of instruments of torture. I squirmed. Brad paced. With the desk officer so close, we didn't feel comfortable talking about Celeste's situation, and after one look at the unappealing contents of the snack machine, I almost hoped that Celeste was served the storied jail fare of black bread and gruel.

The door opened to admit a silver-haired man impeccably dressed in a chalk-striped suit complete with a silk pocket square—definitely not off a department-store rack—and carrying a brushed leather brief case stuffed with law tomes and file folders. Danford T. Chatsworth, Esquire, had arrived.

After checking in with the desk officer, Chatsworth came over to us. "Are you here in regard to Dr. Farnsworth?" he asked.

We introduced ourselves. The two men shook hands, and the attorney walked over to the chair next to Brad. Before Chatsworth could sit down, Chief Koenig came down the hall from his office. Billy was in full uniform, service ribbons and all, and greeted the attorney.

"I'm Bramble Chief of Police William Koenig," he said, adding, "but you can call me Billy."

"How do you do, er, Billy," said Chatsworth, handing one of his business cards to Billy. "Is there a place where we can talk?" He cocked his head in our direction and added, "Privately?"

The two went into one of the conference rooms and shut the door. "Guess we'll have to wait." Brad sat down. I had no intention of missing out on what was being said. Keeping out of the desk policeman's range of vision, I leaned against the wall next to the conference room door. Brad shook his head in disbelief, which didn't stop him from asking, "What are they saying, Meg?"

"Shh." I cut my eyes over to the desk where the police officer was talking with someone on the phone. "I'll tell you in a bit," I mouthed.

I tried to look nonchalant as I eavesdropped as best I could, but I didn't need to strain to hear what the chief and Chatsworth were saying—especially the attorney, his stentorian courtroom voice booming at Billy. When the men seemed to be drawing their conversation to a close, I returned to my plastic chair. "You probably heard a lot of it, Brad."

Brad nodded. "Chatsworth wasn't using his 'inside voice,' that's for sure."

"From my listening post, I heard that the magistrate and her backup are both unavailable for the next couple of weeks. So far, there's been no word from the county prosecutor about bringing charges. As Chatsworth quoted several times from a couple of the law references he brought along, Billy became more and more intimidated. And less and less eager to charge Celeste with murder.

"The attorney made the point over and over that there's no 'smoking gun' or real proof—as yet, anyway—linking her to the drugs in Arch's system. So after much hemming and hawing by Billy Koenig, he agreed to release Celeste as long as she stayed in Bramble—except for going to work—so she'll probably move in with Gloria." I gave a fist pump. "Yes!"

Brad stared at me. "I'm amazed. I've been in law enforcement for all these years. I'm happy for Celeste, but, Meg, She's a prime suspect in a murder inquiry."

I squeezed his arm and said, "Brad, you forget. You're in Bramble."

***

"Well, she's well-known and respected in the area, so that's in her favor," Brad said, speaking of Celeste Farnsworth as he reached for another sandwich from the plate on my kitchen table. "A lot will depend on whether any substantial evidence is found tying her to Arch's death.

"And," he continued, "I can attest that she planned to come in today and make a voluntary statement. If she is charged and surrenders her passport, there's a good chance that bail will be granted. Maybe have to wear an electronic ankle band. Much of it depends on the charge. If the prosecutor's office goes with first-degree murder, I'm sure she will stay inside the Seminole County jail until her trial is over."

"First-degree murder! Let's hope it doesn't come to that." I thought for a moment. "Brad, Arch took all her money. And the Wellness Center may suspend her, maybe without full pay. How can she come up with bail money?"

"Good thought, Meg. What about her sister, Gloria? She might be able to mortgage her house or take out a loan on her business, but I'd like to see if we can avoid having her do that." He paused. "I may have some sources that might help us. And Craig Montrose works with investment concerns all over the world. Maybe there's something he can suggest."

"For all we know, Gloria may not have enough funds in any case. She's already on the hook for that attorney," I said as I finished my sandwich and the rest of my Diet Coke. "Brad, while you're contacting Craig and other finance guys, I'm going to call Sally and see if she's available to go with me to go to Gloria's and talk with her and Celeste. On our way home, I had noticed Gloria's car was in her driveway, so she's home. I don't know if we can help, but I'm sure they need some reassurance and support from friends."

Chapter 19

I called Gloria to let her know that Sally and I would like to stop in. "Oh, Meg, that's so sweet of you both. It would be good to talk to someone who actually cares what happens to Celeste." Sally agreed to meet me at Gloria's house that afternoon.

I looked at the clock. Not enough time to write an article to send to Harry Josten. Not enough time for any of the household chores I'd been putting off. I made a desultory attempt to tidy the kitchen, wiping the counters and putting dishes away. Perhaps I should bring something to eat to Gloria's. Bramble Lutheran's church ladies, like their counterparts in all faiths, always brought casseroles with them on their visits to parishioners—I often wondered if they kept a collection of one-dish meals in their freezers, ready to go at a moment's notice. An unopened box of cookies in the pantry caught my eye. I checked the expiration date and they were still okay to eat. Of course they were. Cookies don't have time to get stale at my house. They would just have to do.

Sally was pulling into Gloria's driveway as I arrived on foot, carrying my package of store-bought cookies. Sally opened the trunk of her car and lifted out—a casserole.

Gloria greeted us at the door and motioned us inside. She'd been crying and her eyes were bloodshot to almost the same color as her hair. "Thank you so much," she sniffed and dabbed at her nose. We handed her our food offerings and Gloria trotted off to her kitchen to put them away.

Celeste was seated on one end of the sectional sofa and looked up as we entered. A box of Kleenex was on the table beside her and a small wastebasket containing used tissues on the floor at her feet. To put it bluntly, she looked terrible. She was pallid and drawn, and looked like she'd lost weight in the short time since Brad and I were at her home. She wore an old chenille bathrobe, presumably one of her sister's as it was much too large for her. A far cry from a peignoir, but way more comforting. A blanket was tucked loosely around her legs. "Hi," she said, her voice weak. "I'd get up, but…" Her voice trailed off.

"Celeste, don't get up." Sally said. "You look comfortable right there." We walked over and gave her a hug.

Gloria's home was a complete contrast from what I'd expected. Given her bright-colored hair and her fondness for strong pinks and purples used in the decor of Gloria's Glamour salon, I was surprised by the neutral hues of tans, soft yellows, and greens in her home. Before we sat down, I noticed a small oil painting of a group of children playing in the sand, a gentle ocean rippling behind them. Sally and I walked over to look at it.

"Wow!" Celeste's signature was in the corner in block capitals. "Celeste painted this."

"It's delightful," Sally said.

"Yes, Celeste gave it to me one Christmas," said Gloria, who had returned from the kitchen and bore a tray holding a bottle of wine, glasses, and a plate of crackers. "As you may recall, she studied art at Rutgers before switching to medicine at Johns Hopkins."

Now that she mentioned it, I did recollect Gloria telling me about her sister when Celeste moved here to accept the position at the Walnut Creek Wellness Center. I foraged in my brain and remembered, "And she designed your new business cards, right?"

"That's right," replied Gloria.

"Hey, you two!" called Celeste. "I'm in the room, you know. I can hear you."

We laughed. It was good to see a bit of humor surfacing. It even gave Celeste a bit more color in her cheeks than when we first came in.

Gloria pulled a chair over to the oversized coffee table in front of the sectional, poured the wine, and passed out paper plates and napkins. Sally kicked off her shoes and tucked her feet under her at one end of the couch. "Let's review what we know and where we are," she suggested. She looked at the three of us. "And what we can do. That's the important part."

I reached into my purse and pulled out pencil and paper. "I'll be the secretary. Where shall we start? With the evidence?"

Sally said, "Keep in mind I need to catch up with what you already know."

"So...the beginning." I turned to Celeste. "Are you going to be okay with us going over Arch's death and so on?"

Celeste nodded. "Don't worry about me. I almost feel like I never really knew him." She dabbed at her eyes. "When I think about all of this...and him...it's almost as if I'm thinking or talking about a dear friend I once knew." She drew a long breath. "And, in a way, I guess it is."

"Okay," said Sally, "but tell us if it's getting to be too much…too painful…whatever."

Celeste nodded again.

"So," I began, "The coroner told me Arch was killed by an overdose of morphine administered in coffee. Celeste, what can you tell us about morphine? I know it's made from opium—Sherlock Holmes gave me that bit of knowledge. And I know it's deadly and prevalent on the streets."

"Legally, drugs containing morphine are available only by prescription," Celeste began. "Pharmaceutical use of pure morphine is rare; it's usually combined with other substances and sold in drugs such as codeine."

"I've taken codeine when I had a bad cough I couldn't shake," said Sally. "And I had to practically sign my life away for the prescription."

"Right," said Celeste. "Codeine's a controlled drug, which means it must be signed for and there are no automatic refills. For people in extreme pain, such as those with advanced cancer, chronic pain, or catastrophic injury, morphine is given in much stronger compounds such as oxycodone hydrochloride, known better as OxyContin." She sighed. "That's one of the major strikes against me. As an M.D., I can write prescriptions for narcotics but I don't remember ever doing so. I help people *recover* from their drug habit, for Pete's sake. I can't imagine a case where I would write a prescription for any highly addictive drug. And people suffering from a high degree of pain wouldn't be coming to me. They'd go to their regular doctor or surgeon.

"So, I guess what I'm saying is that technically, I could've obtained the drug and given it to Arch. I hadn't noticed any signs of suicidal thoughts or plans, so it's unlikely he used it to kill himself." She looked at us. "I really do believe I would've seen the signs. And Arch hadn't any injuries or health issue that would require an opioid. Just the usual aches and pains. Maybe an aspirin or two…"

"Would he have noticed if his coffee tasted off?" I asked.

"I doubt it." Celeste gave a wry smile. "Arch kidded that he should become one of my patients so he could lick his addiction to caffeine. He made the coffee whenever he was at my house and he took an insulated cup of it with him to work. With Norton's coffee bar so close to the construction site, I'm sure Arch had a few cups during the day and picked up a cup for the drive home. The way he gulped coffee, even if it wasn't fresh or had gone cold, I don't think he would've cared even if it tasted a little odd."

Sally asked, "You said 'legally,' Celeste. What about illegal sources of morphine?"

"On the street, availability of narcotics of all kinds is increasing. So many more deaths these days."

"Have any of your patients told you where they got their drugs?"

"I'm afraid not. Their primary concern is getting clean, getting their families off their backs. They're desperate to avoid any contact with their dealers—let alone put the police onto them. Keep in mind, too, that the illegal purchase of a controlled substance is punishable by law, so that, and fear of reprisal from their supplier, keeps addicts from naming names. Use of illegal drugs is growing exponentially but, so far, Bramble has had very few problems with it."

"And you've pretty much said Arch wasn't suicidal. He didn't use anything other than over-the-counter meds for pain."

"Right," replied Celeste.

"So it was murder," I said. "And the source of the narcotic unknown."

"And me with a motive, the means, and plenty of opportunities."

Gloria, in a burst of anger, said, "That man took every cent my sister had, all her investments, everything. And gambled it away. As far as I'm concerned, he got what he deserved—but Celeste didn't do it!"

"I was such a fool!" said Celeste. "I loved him. We had so much fun together, shared interests…I trusted…" Tears welled up in her eyes. "When we were at The Heron that night you saw us, I just lost it. He was so nonchalant about it. And, of course, there were other witnesses to it all." She reached for the box of tissues.

Silence spooled out as we sipped our wine and nibbled on the crackers. Gloria drew Celeste to her and her sister leaned her head on Gloria's shoulder.

I broke the silence. "Celeste, you mentioned that Arch found notes in his truck with some sort of death threat," I said.

"Oh, yes." Celeste brightened. "Actually, I have one of them. I planned to give it to my attorney, but forgot to." Celeste reached over to the end table for her purse and dug around in it. She pulled out a rumpled piece of paper, which she placed on the coffee table so we could all see it. "Here it is."

YOU ARE MARKED FOR DEATH*!*

The message was neatly printed in block capitals in ink on a piece of white paper, which was torn on two edges. We passed it around, taking turns to examine it.

"How many other ones did he get?" asked Sally.

"I'm not sure," answered Celeste. "I only saw this one. Although Billy Koenig said they found one in Arch's truck."

"I'll talk to Billy and see what I can find out," I said, adding it to my mental list. "Maybe there were fingerprints on it."

"Oh!" exclaimed Celeste, "I didn't think about that." She pointed to the note on the table. "I suppose it's too late for this one. We've all handled it." We all looked sheepish.

I could've kick myself. I knew better than to handle potential evidence.

"I'll give you a plastic baggie to put it in," said Gloria. "You can take it with you, Meg, when you go to see Chief Koenig."

"It would be best to give it to your attorney, Celeste," I said, "and let him decide what to do with it. I'm afraid Billy might take it as proof that Celeste wrote them to cover up her crime—and still had one in her possession."

"Good thought. I'll do that."

Sally said, "We've got the *alleged* motive—Arch absconding with Celeste's money. And we've got part of the means: morphine.

"Part of the means?" asked Gloria.

"What about the coffee the drugs were in?" asked Sally, looking a bit triumphant.

"I saw Arch toss his coffee cup in the trash at the work site before he got into his truck. I think it was one of Norton's, but I wasn't close enough to be sure," I said. I thought about the coffee counter at Norton's. "Phil Norton has a coffee station just inside the door of his store. Workmen–or anyone else—can come in and get coffee to take with them. Customers put their money in a coffee can, so no cashier needs to handle all those dollar bills and small change. Kind of an honor system."

"Well, after our argument at The Heron the night before, Arch dropped me off at my condo. That was the…" Celeste's voice wobbled. "the last time I saw him."

"So his Thermos was still with him the next day," said Sally, "but you had no chance to tamper with it."

"Good point," commented Gloria.

"Where do you think Arch went after driving you home?" I asked.

"Probably bunked with his friend, Martin Bryson, in his trailer. Arch still had some odds and ends at Martin's. Keeping stuff there until we found a bigger place to live and were married." Celeste pulled another tissue from the box and dabbed at her nose.

Sally asked, "Celeste, did Arch usually lock his truck?"

"Not unless he had building materials or something else of value inside. Before you ask, he parked his truck outside in my townhouse parking lot each night." She sat upright. "Of course, he wasn't at my house the night before he…"

"Exactly! For the life of me, Celeste, I can't see how you could've drugged his coffee. He would've had any coffee made at your house on his way to work after staying at your house. Same with any coffee slipped into his unlocked truck. That evening, he went directly from The Heron to Martin's, so he probably finished off any coffee—if any—left in his truck.

"If Martin or someone tampered with Arch's coffee after that—either in Arch's Thermos or in a cup—Arch would've drunk it on his way to the construction site the next morning and died on his way into town."

"I'll visit Chief Billy and see what I can learn about the container holding Arch's coffee."

"Oh, Meg, thank you so much!" exclaimed Celeste. "I feel better already."

Sally looked at us. "Can we think of anything else about the coffee?"

We shook our heads.

"Then," she said, "we need to brainstorm what to do next."

"Celeste, you mentioned that Arch gambled with a pretty tough crowd. Someone should find out more about who they are. Maybe Brad has some FBI connections. I'll ask him."

"I'm glad you clarified that, Meg," said Gloria. "I thought about looking in to it, but then I had visions of being bashed on the head in an alley outside a gambling den." She laughed and patted her curls. "It would spoil my hairdo."

Her remark tweaked my risibility. I stuffed it down with a cracker. As I wiped my mouth, Sally asked, "Besides patients using it, who else has access to legal opioids?"

Celeste replied, "Other doctors, pharmacists, drug dealers, hospital workers. I would be willing to check with hospital staff, but…"

"Honey, you're under surveillance right now," Gloria said. "Better leave that with the others."

"I'll check on Phil Norton," I offered. The three women stared at me in surprise. "Yikes!' I said, "I don't think he had anything to do with it. I'll just ask if he remembers any other details or if there are other incidents that might shed some light on this."

"Kim Winters is a nurse at Bramble Memorial," said Sally. "She's on the Millennium Arts Committee. I can ask her about any discrepancies in the hospital dispensary inventories."

Gloria said, "Any ideas about how to reach drug dealers?"

"I'll put that on my list to talk with Billy about," I said. "As our Chief of Police, he must know something about who might be pushing drugs in the area. I'll also ask Brad about anything he might know about illegal drug trafficking."

We finished the rest of the wine, each of us lost in thought. "I can't think of anything more we can do at this point," said Gloria. We nodded our agreement.

Sally said, "Gloria, you know Craig and Brad are looking into ways to ease the financial situation for you and Celeste, if worse comes to worst and you are charged with, er, something."

Gloria reached for a tissue and made an attempt to wipe the tears that rolled freely down her face. "I don't know what to say. You're all so kind to us…"

"What goes around comes around, Gloria." I said, a little teary myself. "You've been helping people like Charlene Pullen. Now it's your turn."

Chapter 20

A few days later

At last, the police released the Bramble Community Center building site, after scouring it for clues to Arch's death. Time was slipping by, and the Millennium Arts Committee decided to meet at the work site to ascertain how far along work had progressed on the buildings. It was one of those unusual early summer days, a "Goldilocks Day"—not too hot, not too cold—just right. Brad, wearing a hard hat, stood inside the fence near the shed used to store small equipment and supplies, and was talking with Martin Bryson, Arch's friend, now in charge of the project. Outside the fence, Kim Winters, Millie Pullen, and Cam Podolski, who had the haggard look of a new father spending a lot sleepless nights, were going over a list Kim held. Sally, Celeste, and I stood a bit apart from the group.

Just then, Gladys Koenig came up to the three of us. She stopped. Her mouth in a twisted rictus of malevolence, she glared at Celeste and snarled, "I can't believe you have the nerve to show up here," she sneered, "although I suppose we won't be seeing you much longer, *Doctor* Farnsworth. It's just a matter of time until my Billy puts you in jail where you belong—and where you should be right now. I'll see the building another time. I'm particular about the company I keep. I'm leaving!"

Gladys turned and flounced off, leaving us gawking at her retreating back. I exclaimed, "Just ignore her, Celeste. Guess she doesn't know she's not an airline and doesn't need to announce her departure." Sally and Celeste gave faint smiles at my pitiful attempt at levity and Sally patted Celeste's arm.

Martin Bryson came over to the gate and admitted us. He was of average height, but with a powerful build. He wore a neatly trimmed beard, and when he smiled at us, a gold tooth shone among his front teeth. He carried a mesh bag like those used by coaches to carry several soccer balls, but filled with hard hats.

"Everyone must wear a hard hat," he said as he gave one to each of us, "and keep them on all the time you're here. Don't want any more—anyone hurt."

He showed us how to adjust the straps and we tramped through the dirt and gravel toward the main building, the former Victorian home. Martin reported that the inside work was completed except for painting and refinishing the floors. The landscaper is coming next week to put down sod and plant some bushes. "All the permits were okayed," Martin said, "so everything's ready to go." He paused. "Shall we go in?"

Martin flipped a switch inside the entry and the large chandelier overhead blazed to life. It had survived the Memory Gardens fire and was back from being cleaned. All of us, even Millie Pullen, stared up at it, our mouths open in awe.

We walked through the downstairs and admired the woodwork, waxed and polished, the chandelier giving the dark wood a rich glow. The beveled, leaded-glass mullioned windows cast small rainbows of light into the room. A two-person elevator had been installed next to the massive staircase leading up to what had been the offices and private rooms of the former owner.

"I can't believe there wasn't damage to the woodwork and that magnificent staircase," I remarked to Martin.

"Actually, there was extensive damage to the banister and some of the door frames," he replied. "Arch was over here many nights restoring them. He had been a sculptor as well as a wood worker, you know, and it sure came in handy."

When we were outside again, Martin walked us over to the structures that had housed the mortuary and crematorium. "The plans call for these to be torn down, so we'll do that next. The insides are gutted, but it will be a while before we get to it. We first want to get the grounds and the main building spiffy for the grand opening."

"That's fine, Martin," said Sally. "We haven't decided on what we want to do with this area. There's enough space now in the parking lot for booths and concession stands for the Arts Festival, so don't feel you have to rush." Sally beamed at him. "Martin, this is wonderful. So professional, yet so creative."

A smile lit up his dark face. "Thank you, but, well, that was mostly Arch, ma'am. He had a flare for seeing how things could be. A visionary, you might say."

Sally said, "Still, Martin, you've also left your mark on this project too. Dare I ask about cost?"

"Well," the builder said slowly, "there were some issues…"

We braced for bad news.

"Two of the doorways upstairs needed to be widened to comply with accessibility codes, and there was the elevator, which we hadn't counted on costing so much. And then…"

A fist of dismay gripped my stomach.

Bryson grinned. "Your faces! I can't do this to you, keep you in suspense any longer. And then…thanks to Miss Millie here…"

We turned to look at Millie Pullen. Her eyes were cast down, but her mouth formed a rare smile.

"She wrote two grant proposals for funding the doorway changes and the elevator." Martin paused. "The grants were successful—we met our budget!"

The group cheered, pumped Millie's hand, and thumped her on back a few times. "Stop, stop! Mercy!" she said. "I just wanted to do more than just take minutes. I love this town, you know."

Chapter 21

Brad suggested we all "repair" to The Heron for lunch, with Millie Pullen and Martin Bryson as our guests. We were so thrilled and delighted with the news, we even laughed at Brad's pun. After we placed our orders, Cam asked Martin, "How did you meet Arch?"

"We knew each other in college. Oregon. Odd, really. He was in fine arts and I majored in engineering, We were paired in a random draw for a student pinochle tournament. Before you ask, we didn't win." He chuckled. "In fact, we were so terrible, we were eliminated in the first round. Oh, well. At least we didn't spoil anyone else's chances.

"After we graduated, we got jobs in the area, partied, dated, the usual bachelor things. Arch was a brilliant sculptor and a graduate assistant at the university. I started as a draftsman for an architectural firm, but as a Black man, I knew I wouldn't be designing bridges or housing complexes any time soon, if ever. Arch heard they needed guys to work on the Alaska pipeline and the pay was amazing. I was surprised when he decided to give up his art, but he said he felt trapped in a relationship, needed a change, maybe get some fresh ideas. I eventually followed him there.

"So when—or how—did Arch convince you to come to Bramble?" Brad asked.

"Actually, it was the other way around. Alaska is beautiful beyond any description I could give, and everyone should visit there. I'd been injured at work and while I recovered, had some time to think. Decided I'd had enough of freezing nights and long hours of winter darkness. At about the same time, I inherited a mobile home in the park outside Bramble, so here I am. A few months later, Arch contacted me—he'd had his fill of Alaska too, and he came back down to the 'Lower Forty-Eight' and moved in with me. I'll always be indebted to Arch for hiring me. Working with him on the Community Center was a godsend for me. I love what I do." Martin got up from the table, "By the way, Celeste, I have a box of Arch's things at the trailer. What should I do with it?"

"I don't know," she answered. "He never told me much about his family or his past."

"I can run over there sometime soon, Martin, and get the box," I offered. "Celeste, you can let me know if and when you want to go through it."

Lunch over, Millie and Martin left for their respective jobs. I caught Martin at the door and asked him if Arch had stayed with him the night before he was murdered. "Yes, he did, Meg. Some sort of argument with his girlfriend."

"Do you remember if he made coffee and took some to work in another cup?"

Martin stared at me. "What do you mean, Meg?"

"The drugged coffee was in a cup from Norton's Drug Store."

Martin put his hands on his hips. "I resent what you're implying, Meg. I had nothing to do with Arch's death."

I waited. "But in answer to your question, "Yes, he brought that cup in with him and filled it from my pot the next morning."

"I'm so sorry, Martin. We're just trying to find out what happened. Celeste is their main suspect, and it's impossible to believe she did it."

"Apology accepted. But, Meg," he added, "be careful. Arch ran with some tough guys, and before you ask, I don't know who they were. Let's just say that not everyone loved him. And not everyone will take kindly to the kind of questions you seem to be asking. Be careful."

Was Martin warning me or threatening me? I shook off my thoughts, went back inside, and sat down with Sally, Celeste, and Brad. Kim Winters and Dr. Podolski had already headed back to the hospital.

The Heron was quiet except for staff moving through the restaurant to reset for the evening diners. Jon and Louis came up to us. "Hi!" said Jon. "Sorry we missed Kim and Cam. We saw you out here, but were rushed off our feet in the kitchen."

"You all looked happy. Some kind of celebration?" asked Louis.

We recounted our tour of the Community Center and the successful performance to budget.

"Wow! That's marvelous!" said Jon. "What's going to happen to the other buildings?"

"The mortuary and the crematorium will be razed," replied Sally, "after the current project is completed. I haven't given up on the idea of building a small theater there, but it will be a while before we're at that point."

"I can see opening night at the old crematory," said Jon, sweeping his hand through the air as if reading a marquee, "*Some Like It Hot.*"

"Or theater in the mortuary, *The Ice Man Cometh,*" Louis chimed in.

"You two are too much," said Celeste. A brief smile crossed her face. "You really know how to cheer up a girl."

"Darling, we heard about Arch, of course," Louis said. "Jon and I are so terribly sorry."

Celeste was using her napkin to wipe a tear from her cheek. I told the two men about Gladys Koenig's verbal attack at the building site.

"Dear lady," said Jon to Celeste, "don't let that ogress get to you. I'd be grumpy too if I had to sleep with Billy Koenig every night."

***

"I didn't want to get into it with the others," Brad said after Jon and Louis returned to the kitchen, "but I talked with Frieda Koenig and found out more about why the payrolls were sometimes late getting to the workmen.

"Evidently, the payroll was deposited into a special account at the bank for that purpose. Only three people were signatories: Freddie Squared and Arch Donegal. Arch logged the men's hours and reported them to Frieda, who wrote the checks and handled the tax forms and so forth. So far so good. But then, she gave the checks to Arch to distribute to his men.

"Arch held the checks. He couldn't cash them, of course, since they were payable to others. So he wrote checks on the payroll account to himself and cashed them to cover his gambling debts. He watched the balance on the bank account and when the next payroll was transferred to it by Frieda, Arch would give out the checks to the workers. Since the guys were paid weekly, there was usually—usually, not always—enough time for the next payroll to be deposited before the checks Arch wrote to himself cleared the account.

"Frieda is a sharp businesswoman, so when she set up the account, she made sure that checks over a certain amount required two signatures. Arch got around this by forging her husband's signature to add to his own, knowing Fred rarely, if ever, got involved with the finances of the village."

I shared what I'd learned from Martin Bryson.

"I'll give a couple of my FBI buddies a call and see if gambling in this area is on their radar. The Treasury is always interested, since gamblers rarely, if ever, declare their gambling income or losses to the IRS."

***

Walking into the sunshine of late afternoon, we went our separate ways: Sally to the library to supervise a new shipment of books; Celeste to Gloria's home to telephone the Wellness Center's director and make an appointment to talk with him; and Brad to the village hall to catch up on paperwork for the MAC. I decided to walk over to Norton's and find out more about the pharmacy's supply of narcotics.

The bell above the shop door jingled as I entered, and Phil Norton looked up from the cashier's counter and smiled. "Hey, Meg! What brings you in today?"

"I'm trying to help Celeste clear her name."

He looked at me, his eyes enormous, magnified by his Coke-bottle lenses. "You know I'll help in any way I can, Meg."

I recounted our tour of the Community Center and Millie Pullen's surprising role in helping the project stay solvent.

"That's terrific news, Meg—and I was ready for some good news, after the whole thing with Arch Donegal. It's touch and go. People are worried about yet another murder in Bramble. Arch almost always walked over during the day to get a cup or two, and after work to get a cup to take with him for his drive back to Walnut Creek. That man drank a lot of coffee! Arch was a local hero, what with his work on the Lutheran Church addition, and then on the Community Center. And folks liked him.

"There are fewer people coming in for coffee now that the word is out that it was our coffee that was drugged." Phil sighed. "Selling the coffee and handling addictive drugs here at the store is a hard combination to get around. The police were here asking me about it. I'll tell you what I told them. I don't get many prescriptions for morphine, so I don't stock stuff like OxyContin or codeine. If I do need to provide it, I contact one of the big drug store chains in Walnut Creek or my usual supply company. Opiates and opioids—people pretty much use the terms interchangeably—are controlled substances, so there are forms to fill out and file. I've filled a few prescriptions over the years for codeine, especially in the flu season. The last prescription I filled for any other opioid—OxyContin, in that case—was for Bert Schmidt."

I stared at Phil.

"He had a terrible accident in his garage. He was working on the engine of a car, but the catch on the hood was faulty, and it slammed down on his arm. Bert was lucky it wasn't his head under the hood. Bert was taken to Bramble Memorial and they prescribed the OxyContin. The pain must've been something else. For a while, he was afraid he'd lose his arm. Had to have a couple more surgeries to restore most of the function in his arm and hand."

"I didn't know that," I said.

"It was a little bit before you moved here. I looked up my records. I only filled one 30-day prescription for time-release capsules for him and, like I said, it was several years ago. Long expired."

"Does OxyContin lose its strength after it expired? Is it dangerous then?"

Phil gave me a sharp look. "Don't go down that path, Meg. With the seriousness of his accident, Bert would've used up all those pills long ago."

"Good to know, Phil," I said. I hated to think Bert Schmidt murdered Arch, but he could've obtained another prescription from another doctor and filled it at another pharmacy. Or kept a few pills just in case his arm acted up.

"Always good to see you, Meg," Phil said, then added, "Please be careful, Meg. Someone murdered Arch Donegal. You don't want that someone alarmed by your questions."

That was the second such warning I'd received that day.

***

I looked up at the sky. Not a cloud to be seen. A good day to get my car washed.

After I filled up my gas tank, I pulled my car around to the car wash. Bert Schmidt came over and opened the car door for me. "Hi, Meg! Full-service wash and wax?"

"Yep." Bert drove my car into the car wash and set the controls. I joined him in the steamy narrow corridor with windows where we could watch the car being washed.

"How's your arm, Bert?" I gave an inward groan. Nothing like a subtle start.

If Bert was surprised at my question, he hid it well. "Thanks for asking, Meg." He swung his arm back and forth. "I lost some range of motion, and it hurts when there's rain coming, but other than that, it's fine."

"Glad to hear it." We went on to talk about the murder. "Did you know Arch well?" I asked.

"Yeah, he had an account here and came in to have me put band-aids on that truck of his. He ran up quite a bill. One of these guys who lived from paycheck to paycheck, I guess. My accountant says I can write it off as a bad debt on my taxes, but I would rather have the money."

"I'm sorry to hear that, Bert. I guess Arch wasn't the guy we thought he was."

The car emerged from the wash and I watched Bert as he wiped it down and washed the windows. Both his arms moved smoothly. I paid him and went on home.

As I was about to turn in that night, a thought struck me: if Bert has pain in his arm before it rains, would running the car wash have the same effect? Of course, he was in the car wash today for only a short time. Normally, Bert wouldn't be running the wash for long stretches. His assistant usually ran the car wash, but today was his day off. I thumped my pillow. I thought back to when Bert towed Cam's car out of the lake. He didn't take money for it, so he must not be desperate. And he was planning to write off what Arch owed him as a bad debt. But he would rather have the money. My pillow took a few more punches before I drifted off to sleep.

Chapter 22

Late May 1999

The ordinary things that comprise the mainstays of life filled my time. I forced myself to begin my ordinary spring cleaning, delayed by the not-so-ordinary murder. Okay, admittedly, murder is on its way to being a frequent occurrence in Bramble. Minerva remained wary of me and crouched under the bed, out of the way of the demon vacuum cleaner, while I washed windows, made minor repairs, and, remembering my chat with Phil, put my expired medications in a bag to turn in at the police station.

I gathered my resolve and opened the clothes closet. Pants, shirts, blazers, and skirts in three different sizes hung on the rods. I fought the still, small voice telling me that if I lost weight, I'd have nothing to wear. I ignored the voice. If I lost weight, I could buy new, celebratory clothes. I filled two large bags with cast-offs. I turned my gaze to the clothes in my laundry basket, where they had been for months. Not today. I would rest on my laurels.

Time to write my next "Miss Polly's Opinion" column. I sighed as I opened my laptop. Harry Josten was right about things changing. Even the questions that my "gentle readers" wrote to me about differed from the topics submitted just a few years ago. No more questions about seating arrangements at dinner parties, the correctness of embossed wedding invitations, or how to deal with a quarrelsome neighbor. Readers now asked Miss Polly for advice in dealing with domestic abuse, how to know if their youngsters are using drugs, and how to handle the effects on their children of the coarse language and graphic violence on television.

I sighed again and began opening the manila envelopes sent from the paper, containing readers' messages, each given a code number for filing. Those letters dealt with, I attacked another sign of change— the growing queue on my computer of e-mails from readers. I soon e-mailed Harry enough material to use in the next several weeks and the code numbers of those pieces of correspondence needing to be brought to the attention of law enforcement or social services. My lower back was complaining. I'd done enough for the day. I stretched. Just one more thing to do.

I sent Harry a summary of the recent events in Bramble—the debate, plans for the Community Center, and, of course, the murder—and received an immediate reply from him and a third warning: "I see Bramble's still doing its bit to decrease the surplus population. Please keep me informed. Seriously, Meg, for heaven's sake, stay safe!"

***

Once again, I visited the police station. Chip Kelly was at the desk. "Hi, Ms. Smyth. How can I help you?"

"Chip! I haven't seen you in an age. Seems just a short while ago that you and your folks rented the house next door to me in the summer. How are you?"

"Just fine. Actually, more than fine. You know Barbara Wilcox and I are getting married this fall." His gray eyes sparkled.

"Congratulations, Chip! I'm happy for both of you. I saw her at The Heron recently, and she didn't mention it. I'll grill her when I see her next."

Chip laughed. "We just got engaged last week, so don't be too hard on her."

"I'll keep that in mind."

He consulted a log book in front of him. "I see you have an appointment with Chief Koenig. You can go on back to his office. His receptionist is away on vacation."

"Thanks, Chip."

Billy Koenig's office door was open and I tapped lightly on it.

"Meg, come in, come in," he said. "We're going to have to give you a desk here pretty soon, you're here so often. And what can I do for you today?"

"Oh, I have a few questions. As usual."

"Fire away," Billy said.

"Arch Donegal's murder. Did you find the container with the tampered coffee?"

"Funny you should ask. I have it right here. Just back from the county forensics lab." He held up a sealed plastic evidence bag containing a coffee cup with one of Norton's sayings, 'Stay Grounded' on it.

"Where did you find it? In Arch's truck?"

Billy confirmed my theory. "No. At the building site. In the trash."

"I saw him toss one in the trash can next to where he was speaking to his crew before driving away."

"Thank you, Meg. That's real helpful."

"Did they find his Thermos?"

"Yeah, there were traces of coffee in it, but no drugs. The county guys did find something else."

"What? Where?"

"A note. In Arch's truck." Billy grunted as he pushed himself out of his desk chair. "Tell you what, Meg. Come with me. I gotta put this cup in our evidence room. It's right down the hall." He walked ahead of me and stopped at a door at the end of the corridor. "Here we are." He selected a key from the ring attached to a chain on his belt and opened the door. He clicked the light switch and the fluorescent fixture on the ceiling flickered on. The room was lined with shelves holding carefully marked bankers' boxes. He lifted one of the boxes, signed a log attached to its cover, and brought it to a large table under the ceiling bulb, opened it, and dropped the evidence bag inside. He held up another evidence bag containing a slip of paper cut on each end. On it were the block letters:

YOU ARE MARKED FOR DEATH!

Without removing it from the bag, which, even in the Bramble police department, wasn't going to happen, the printing and the paper looked similar to the one

Celeste was going to give to her lawyer. To my untrained eye, it looked to be written by the same person.

I recalled the scene at Wallace Arnhart's shop the morning after he was beaten up. "There was something about a note at the Bushel O'Bargains?"

"How did you hear that, Meg? I should deputize you."

I prodded. "So was there a note of some kind?"

Billy walked over to the shelves, pulled out another box, and withdrew an evidence bag. The note in it, written in block capitals, was like the others, the paper torn at each end:

YOU ARE MARKED FOR DEATH*!*

I stood in the hallway as Billy initialed the log, returned the box, turned off the light, shut and locked the door. On our way back to his office, he said, "Anyone could've spiked that coffee, Meg. The crew, the townsfolks, anyone. He didn't usually lock the truck. He once laughed and told me he was hoping someone would steal it so the insurance company would have to pay for a new one.

"Doctor Farnsworth looks like our best bet. Just gotta dig up some more evidence. But I'm pretty sure she did it."

I hoped my annoyance with Billy's foregone conclusion didn't show on my face. "I won't keep you much longer, Chief," I said as he settled himself behind his desk. "Any news on the robbery at Bushel O'Bargains?"

"Not a thing. The guys left no prints. No money or liquor taken."

"'Course Wally was beaten up."

"That was his own fault. Never fight with thugs."

"Speaking of Wally, just one more follow up: any progress in finding out who marked up that flyer of his?"

Koenig's face turned crimson. "We've been a bit busy, Meg."

"I know you have, Chief. I thought as long as I was here…"

"The answer is 'no, we haven't identified who did it.' Arnhart's been bugging me about it almost every day." Koenig forced a smile. "Geez. One flyer. Big deal."

"That's it, Chief." I attempted to soothe his ruffled feathers. "I can't tell you how grateful I am for your help. Never got as much as a 'hello, how are ya?' from the Chicago police."

"Is that so?" Billy beamed. "Well, we're small, but we're mighty."

Chapter 23

Early June 1999

The languid breeze puffing through my bedroom window promised no respite from early summer's hot breath. I could hear birds chirping to one another, and the droning of insects as I languished in bed in that delicious period between sleeping and waking when every prone position is comfortable. Good pillow or old lumpy one, it didn't matter. I could choose to go back to sleep or doze. Just as I drifted into drowsy somnolence, I sat up with a start. There was a MAC meeting today.

The Community Center building was resplendent as I passed it on the way to the meeting in the village hall. Gone were all the odds and ends of building materials, yellow caution tape, and the dumpster from the project. The sod was lush and green. But the show-stopper was the exterior of the Victorian house itself. Its fresh, white paint gleamed in the sunlight. No broken windows. No rotted boards. No missing roofing shingles. It was now the pride of the village.

On my way into the meeting, I met Kim Winters in the hallway. "Hi, Meg. Do you know anything more about Arch's death? Phil Norton told me you were looking into it. Sally Montrose asked me about whether it was difficult to steal opioids from the hospital pharmacy." She frowned. "I understand Sally's motive, but still. The hospital pharmacy might as well be Fort Knox. What Celeste has been going through! Until the murder is solved, she's got this cloud over her—and her career. And even then, there will be people who will always wonder."

"I wish I knew more, Kim," I answered, avoiding telling her what I had learned so far. Changing the subject, I said, "Doesn't the Community Center building look wonderful?"

"Marvelous! Whenever our twins have time, they've been going over there and helping. Keeping their muscles in shape for football, they said." Kim winked. "And earning more date money."

Kim and I entered the meeting together as it was about to start. I took my usual place next to Sally. All the MAC members were present, Gladys Koenig making an obvious passive-aggressive point by turning her body as far away from Celeste Farnsworth as possible, and busying herself with knitting something in garish pink, neon green, and orange yarn for the craft show.

"This meeting shouldn't take too long," said Sally. "We'll need to go to the site again after the vendor booths, concession stands, and exhibit areas are assigned—probably next week. I wanted us to touch base before then in case there are any business issues we need to address.

Brad said, "First, let's give a round of applause to Millie Pullen for obtaining grants that brought our project in at budget."

The group applauded and gave her a standing ovation. Even Gladys put down her knitting and got to her feet. Millie smiled—her smiles were becoming more frequent—and thanked everyone.

"Some of our art exhibits have arrived," said Sally. "As you know, Arch Donegal was on the review committee with Celeste and Meg. To expedite things, would it be okay with all of you if I filled in to look over the entries?" The committee nodded its approval.

"The three of us are going to the library after the meeting. Tom and Todd Winters are coming by to help us uncrate a couple of the larger items." She turned to Kim, "It's so good to have your sons helping us."

"No problem," responded Kim.

The meeting was coming to a close when the redoubtable Frieda Koenig marched in.

"What brings you here, Frieda?" asked Sally. I could tell she suppressed a groan.

"To get straight to the point, I think we need to increase the security at the building site and also during the Bramble Heritage Week itself. After all, our builder was murdered!"

Gladys Koenig put down her knitting and glared at Frieda. "Billy's men have done a wonderful job protecting the work site. There's no need..."

Frieda brushed aside her sister-in-law's interruption and continued, "The need for security is greater now. Heritage Week has grown in leaps and bounds. I contacted the security firm that Arch recommended when the village board called for bids, and the owner is with me today to outline the kind of things we should consider." She opened the door and beckoned to someone outside.

"This is Gabe Wright," she said. A bear of a man filled the doorway. He was a few inches over six feet tall which, together with his dewlaps and bald head, gave him a pugnacious appearance almost stereotypical of a tough security man or private eye. He was well-nourished, with the physique of a large pouter pigeon. He walked over to Frieda.

"Hi, folks," Wright said. He produced a wad of business cards from his jacket pocket and we passed them around. "You have come to the right company. As it says on our card, 'Search no more for the Wright solution.'" He looked around, expecting a chuckle. Getting only blank stares, he cleared his throat and began his presentation.

Wright distributed his proposal and went over it with the committee.

When he stopped—at last—Sally said, "Before we get too bogged down with details, I believe this decision rightly belongs in the hands of the Bramble village board."

"Har, har. That's a good one, Honey," said Wright. "'Wrightly belongs.' Har, har."

Sally gave him a look that could boil water. She started to speak. "Mister..."

Seeing storm clouds gathering on Sally's face, Frieda stood up. "Thank you, Mr. Wright," she said. She tapped him on the shoulder and nudged him toward the door. "I'll be in touch," she said over her shoulder to the committee, thus depriving us from enjoying an acerbic response from "Honey."

***

Sally fumed almost all the way to the library. "'Honey,' indeed!"

Celeste chimed in with, I hate it when one of my patients calls me 'Dear.'"

I was aghast. "You're a doctor!"

"It's amazing how social standards and respect have declined in the time I've been in practice. But," she added, "I don't mind when an elderly man or woman calls me that. It's rather cute."

"Elderly drug addicts?" It was Sally's turn to be aghast.

"Unfortunately, yes, and in growing numbers," replied Celeste. "Many get hooked on pain prescriptions and then can't give them up. Most of those patients don't buy street drugs, but go from doctor to doctor and obtain prescriptions that way."

I was learning more about drugs and addictions than I ever wanted to know. My latent investigative reporter instincts kicked in, and I decided to suggest to Harry a *The Journal-Times* series on elderly addicts in the Chicago. I smiled to myself. He could work on it when he retired.

***

When the three of us reached the library, the Winters twins were already there, deep in a discussion about this year's Bramble High football season. They stood, towering over us, and said, "Hi, Mrs. Montrose, Dr. Farnsworth, Ms. Smyth."

A look passed between the boys. "A lot of people can't tell us apart. Easy. I'm Todd, the handsome one." The boys exchanged another look. "This will help," he said as he pinned on a button with "Tom" printed on it. "Oops! Wrong button."

We laughed. "Bet you've done this a few times before," Sally said.

"Our teachers love it. Except when we, um, mistakenly put on the wrong pin."

The twins exchanged pins and assured us that each was wearing the correct button. Tom hefted the duffel bag he was carrying. "Dad loaned us the tools he thought we might need," he said.

Todd held the door open for us. We entered the cool quiet of the building, and I breathed in the smells that will always mean "library" to me: an indefinable, almost musty presence of bygone eras, of mucilage and inkwells, exercise books and green-ruled penmanship paper.

Sally spoke with her assistant librarian for a few minutes and tugged a library cart out from behind the sprawling marble-topped desk. Tom sprung forward and took the cart and brought it with us as Sally led the way to her office.

Sally's office, usually excruciatingly tidy, was filled with cartons and crates. Celeste and I stood in the doorway as Sally gave directions to the boys. Soon the art exhibits were separated from the multitude of boxes containing new books to be catalogued and shelved, and an unobstructed path to Sally's desk was created.

She said to Celeste and me, "Todd and Tom are coming in later this week to help unpack the new books. So today, we'll just look at what's in these four large crates marked for the Arts Festival. Go ahead and open them, guys. Please, please, be careful!"

The young men soon had the containers open. Three of the containers, shipped directly from the UK and covered with Customs seals and stamps, were from Cyril Atkins, and their interiors were molded to fit each miniature. They were exquisite. Each was accessed by removing the back. One was an English pub, complete with tiny lights, brass harness medallions decorating rough-hewn posts, and taps for "pulling a pint" that actually moved. Another was a country inn, with patchwork quilts on the beds, a kitchen with an Aga stove, and a jolly-faced innkeeper and his plump wife. The third miniature was a police station containing desks, officers in uniforms complete with tiny brass buttons, and a small lock-up holding a rough-looking crook.

"Wow!" said Todd. "Who made these nifty dollhouses?"

I laughed and said, "An Englishman by the name of Cyril Atkins. He's in town and he'd better not hear you call them 'dollhouses.' They're miniatures. All the pieces and figures were made by hand."

"They're really cool. Must take hours to make," said Tom. He looked at his large hands and grinned. "I don't think it's a hobby for me."

"Definitely no problem approving them for the art show. I can see why Cyril objected to these being with the other crafts," said Celeste, with a smile. "But they're so fragile. Let's put them back in their boxes."

The fourth crate was from the University of Oregon and held one of Arch Donegal's sculptures on loan from the university's permanent collection of fine art. We had the twins take apart the crate completely, as we were afraid of marring the sculpture if we moved it past the rough sides of the wooden container.

The piece was a bronze, a little over three feet tall. The subject was a young woman, looking over her shoulder with a slight, teasing smile on her lips. The folds of her clothing were so realistic, I wanted to reach out and touch them.

In the crate were two envelopes. One contained information for contacting the transport company to pack and ship the sculpture back to the university. The other envelope contained a heavy, embossed card with information for use in its display:

Carina

Archer Donegal

bronze

Courtesy: Permanent Collection

University of Oregon

No one spoke. Celeste wiped her eyes. Finally, Sally cleared her throat and asked, "Celeste, do you know who the model was—Carina?"

"I have no idea," she replied. "Probably a life model at the university."

Sally and I exchanged a glance. Models for art classes don't have bronzes named for them.

"It's a stunning piece," said Sally. "We must make it the centerpiece of our show." She walked slowly around the sculpture as she thought about it. "I know! There's a small, round table in the Community Center. We'll drape it in black velvet, put the table beneath the chandelier, and place *Carina* on it!"

I added, "We'll need some way to keep people from touching it. Same with the miniatures and the other art."

"Um…" said Tom. "What about borrowing some velvet ropes and stanchions from the movie theater in Walnut Creek?"

"Yeah," added Todd. "One of the guys on the team works in the projection room on weekends. We can ask him."

"Oh, please do!" said Sally. "We'll be sure keep them safe and sound and return them promptly."

We chattered about the show, our eyes returning again and again to the bronze. "Well," said Sally, "I'd best get back to work. Let's put *Carina* on the table there in the corner where she'll be safe and out of the way." She motioned to the twins, who looked terrified at the thought of moving it. "Don't worry, guys. It won't break."

I crossed fingers of both my hands behind my back.

Chapter 24

Like *Brigadoon,* Bramble was stirring from the sleepy town it usually was. After all, Bramble Heritage Week was right around the corner! Every year, Independence Day was celebrated all week long as part of Heritage Week. This year, before the calendar turned to 2000, Heritage Week was on steroids.

I wandered along Main Street and was agog with amazement. Anything that didn't move—and quite a few things that did—was decorated in red, white, and blue. Fire hydrants—already red, of course—had little American flags attached to those sticks on top marking where the hydrants were when the snow is deep.

Work on the contest for the best-decorated store windows was in full swing—with the winner to be given the privilege of leading the July Fourth parade as its Grand Marshal. A line of customers chatted to one another as they waited on the sidewalk to enter the Fulton hardware store, where a placard outside advertised items for decorating: markers, banners, poster paper, bunting, spray paint, and the like. Sage stood at the door, helping people leaving with their purchases, and indicating that the next person in line could enter. She waved to me as I skirted the crowd.

I marveled at the creativity of the shop windows. My fellow Brambletonians didn't stop at flags and stars. Phil Norton was on a ladder stretching his short arms to attach bunting over his store window in which was a life-sized papier mâché Betsy Ross in her familiar pose with the flag she sewed draped across her lap—but with a cup of coffee in her hand.

"Can I help, Phil?" I asked. "Maybe hold your ladder? Looks a bit unsteady." I grabbed the ladder.

He climbed down the ladder. "Thanks, Meg, but I think I'm done. How's it look?" We both stepped back to admire it.

"Wow! So clever, Phil. I assume Sage made it?"

"It was her idea and she did all the work in my storeroom. It was fun to see it take shape over the chicken wire. She's a marvel. So busy all the time, I sometimes worry about her."

We talked a few minutes more. I continued my saunter down Main Street, crossing the street from time to time to see especially interesting displays and to avoid getting in the way of the kids, brandishing washable spray paint and markers, who had volunteered to decorate windows with patriotic themes.

The Bushel O'Bargains window brought me up short. I stood and admired what had to be another of Sage's artwork. On the window was a detailed replica of the famous *Washington Crossing the Delaware* painting. It was stunning. I moved closer to admire the detail. I stared. Barely noticeable in tiny letters on the hull of the boat was Frieda's campaign slogan.

THE BEST MAN FOR MAYOR IN 2000 IS A WOMAN!

***

Dad was released from in-patient care at the Walnut Creek Wellness Center, and needed only a little more out-patient therapy. My parents vacated the apartment they were renting by the month from the Center, and would stay with me for a while until they determined what to do. Mom apologized over and over about having to share my house, quoting again her "too many women in the house" point of view. I had no worries on that score. Mom and I aren't likely to get in each other's way, since it's the kitchen where most squabbles between women sharing a house take place.

Today, my folks moved into my house. Their apartment near the hospital came furnished, so my parents had only some clothes and toiletries and a few microwaveable items of food to move. It all fit in their rental SUV. Brad and I helped them load the car and then followed them back to my cottage and brought their things to my spare bedroom.

After Brad left, Dad napped on the sofa, while Mom puttered around upstairs. When the noises from upstairs ceased, I opened the door a crack and peeked into their room, and saw that Mom had also succumbed to a nap. I decided to treat myself to a Belly Buster at Max Trent's Liberty Café, which shared a parking lot near the Interstate with the Sleepytime Motel. I left my folks a message saying I was running errands, as I knew my mother would not approve of my luncheon fare.

I snugged my little Toyota between two mammoth eighteen-wheelers and walked across the gravel parking lot to the restaurant. As always, the neon sign remained unrepaired, the A in EAT missing, so the sign flashed E T at irregular intervals. Inside, along with a rack of free publications about flea markets in the area, were sales items aimed at the long-distance trucker market: little cardboard pine-scented air fresheners, chewing tobacco, and greeting cards. The latter were definitely not for when one cared enough to send the very best, most having scantily clad women and the greetings a considerable way beyond suggestive.

A waitress led me to a table made of plasticized wood. She handed me a laminated menu dotted with greasy smears, and a few minutes later, returned with a scratched plastic glass of lukewarm water. "What'll ya have, young lady?" she asked, between cracks of her gum. I continue to wonder why younger people think it's appropriate to call an older woman "young lady." The only ones who ever used that term were my parents when I was truly a young lady and had done something a young lady truly shouldn't have done. My waitress tapped her fingers on her order pad, her jaws ruminating at nearly the speed of sound. I gave her my order.

***

As I made ready to leave, I glanced at the dozens of glass-eyed, dusty stuffed animal heads on the walls. Max Trent came over to my table. He was a good-sized man, evidence he enjoyed his own cooking. His chef's jacket was spotted with residue from menu items. He wore a small chef's hat over his dark hair.

"Meg! You haven't been in here for ages! What's new?" He lowered his voice. "Anything more on Arch Donegal's murder?"

I guess I shouldn't have been surprised at his use of the term "murder," but it still gave me a jolt that Bramble was the site of another killing. "I know nothing," I replied.

"Yeah. I've told my staff not to talk about it here. Spoils business. I mean, the truckers will come in and eat, stay at the motel, no matter what, but we get customers from around the area who want a fine burger, and business has dropped off a bit.

"I see you're admiring my animals." He gestured at the buffalo and rhinoceros, animals that never trod the same continent, now sharing a wall and providing a dubious ambience to the Liberty Café. "That Phil Norton's got a good idea with the sayings on his paper cups. I'm thinking of getting cups made with pictures of my animal heads on them. Whaddya think?"

"It's an idea," I said, trying to sound neutral. The animal trophies were a bit of a joke around Bramble, the rumor mill opining that Max bought all of them at a garage sale.

***

Mom and Dad were both up when I returned home. Mom, predicably, was in the kitchen, cooking. I had made an emergency run to the supermarket the day before, in an attempt to countermand her belief that I lived on condiments and ancient foodstuffs turning against me in the refrigerator. She shook her head when I asked if she needed any help, so I moseyed into the living room where Dad was watching a game show, alternately groaning and shouting advice. I gave him a peck on the cheek and perched on the sofa arm to watch for a bit before I returned to the kitchen.

"Mmm…something smells good," I said.

"I'm making several casseroles," Mom answered. "Busy time coming up with Bramble Heritage Week. Thought we'd freeze them and have quick meals on hand."

"And for emergencies," I said, thinking of Sally's and my visit to Celeste and Gloria.

I avoided the quizzical look from Mom and busied myself setting out plates and silverware for dinner. She wouldn't be pleased to know her daughter brought store-bought cookies to comfort her friends in their time of need.

After dinner, Dad turned in early, and after Mom and I finished loading the dishwasher and tidying up, Mom said, "I have something for you, Meg. She groped around in her tote bag and pulled out an item wrapped in tissue paper. "Ta-da!"

"A teapot!" I exclaimed with false enthusiasm. I was doomed. I could see a tea cozy leitmotif running through my future. Another peccadillo on parade.

"Not just *a* teapot, Meg. It's the one your father made to go with the tea cozy Gae sent you." She dropped her voice to a whisper. "He doesn't know I brought it. He wanted to throw it out. Imagine! Won't he be surprised when he sees his little pot and the cozy on display at the Arts Festival?"

"He sure will." I forced a smile. The teapot was red with a blue not-quite-fitting lid and was, um, somewhat misshapen. I thought of the teapot formed by little girls' arms as they sang, "I'm a little teapot, short and stout."

"Let's see how the cozy looks on it."

I took the cozy from a drawer and plopped it on the teapot. Mom beamed and nearly clapped her hands in joy. "What a dear little thing. And those cute Danish flags. Those took a lot of work, Meg."

"Yes."

"Do you think it's good enough for the crafts display at the festival?"

Recalling the ghastly yarn Gladys Koenig was fashioning into something at the MAC meeting, I replied, "Oh, absolutely. No problem."

Mom handed the items to me. "Put them where we'll be sure to remember to bring them. But don't let your father see them."

"Okay." I walked over to the pantry and found a place for them.

"Speaking of the Arts Festival," said Mom, "when we drove down Main Street on the way here, it looks like everyone's going all-out."

I told Mom about the window decorating contest. "I think one of Sage's creations is sure to win," I said, and described her work at Norton's and Bushel O'Bargains.

"Wallace Arnhart isn't going to be pleased about his window. If he finds the slogan, he will be furious, maybe even fire Sage."

"Let's hope he doesn't see the detail. I only saw it by almost pressing my nose against the glass."

My mother glanced at the kitchen clock. "Goodness! I didn't know it was so late. Off to bed with me."

I wished her good night, turned off the lights, and went outside to sit on one of the lawn chairs. The summer night air was thick and heavy, the other side of the lake shrouded in a foggy veil. It was a long time since I enjoyed the simple joy of the lake and its night sounds. I lingered until drowsiness overcame me and I went inside.

Chapter 25

All of us slept late the next day. Dad was still in bed when Mom and I came downstairs. As we pottered around the kitchen, I noticed that she didn't move as briskly as she once did, her hair was white in places, and her hands were sprinkled with age spots. I wondered again what their plans were for the future. I pushed that thought aside and said, "Mom, I need to get a box or two of Arch's things from his friend, Martin Bryson, today. Why don't we leave Dad here fishing and the two of us drive over today in your SUV to Martin's mobile home and pick up the things?"

"Meg, if you have an ulterior motive, you know I'm not keen about living in a trailer."

"No pressure, no cost, no obligation, no salesman will call. I really do have to pick up Arch's things for Celeste to look through."

Mom sighed. "All right, but—"

"Not to fret. We'll just get the stuff and come back home."

***

We left Dad, wearing his faded canvas hat with fishing lures pinned on it, sitting on a chair at the end of the pier, holding his pole, its line bobbing in the water. Beside him were a cooler with snacks and water, a second cooler with selections from Johnny's Bait Emporium, and his multi-pronged aluminum cane propped against the chair.

The trailer park, Restful Ponds, was about twenty minutes away. Martin was working at the Community Center so he had left a key at the management office for us.

A sign at the entrance directed us to the office located in a grove of trees. I'd seen brochures but was skeptical as to their veracity. True to its description, Restful Ponds was not a bunch of beat-up trailers lined up in rows on acres of concrete. We drove along paved roads lined with well-maintained homes on wooded, landscaped lots. The two namesake ponds shimmered in the sunlight as we approached the park's office.

Mom stayed in the car when I went in the office for the keys. An older woman was pecking at an old, black Smith-Corona typewriter and looked up as I entered. I mentioned we had come to pick up Martin Bryson's keys. She smiled and handed me the keys, along with a map of the park, which she marked with the route to his unit. "Just bring the keys back here when you're finished."

Martin's unit was a single-wide, with a living-dining room, kitchen, two bedrooms, two full baths, and a deck overlooking a stand of dark green evergreens. A large box was on his kitchen table. He had left a message saying that Arch had traveled light and hadn't opened the box since he arrived. The message was written in the fine block printing of a draftsman.

I put the box in the back of the SUV and drove around the park for a few minutes. My mother said little, but I could tell she was better disposed toward trailers—manufactured homes, as they were called now. We dropped off the keys at the office and headed back to my cottage where I carried in the box and shoved it under the shelves in the pantry until Celeste let us know what she wanted us to do with them.

***

Dad was snoozing on the couch in the living room, with Minerva curled up on the back of it. As Mom added pecans, chopped apples, and grapes to her already wonderful chicken salad, Minerva strolled in and eyed the counter. "Don't even think about it!" I warned. She sat and nonchalantly washed a paw in attempt to fool me into thinking the chicken salad held no interest for her.

Mom filled the croissants she had heated and carried them over to the table. I brought in the jug with sun tea we'd left brewing on the porch, and plunked some ice cubes into three tumblers. Dad came in, sat down at the table, and browsed through *The Bramble Buzz*, and Minerva settled herself on his lap to be closer to the chicken.

"So, Meg," said Mom, "what do you know about Arch being murdered?" She pointed to *The Buzz*, its headline screaming "Police Baffled!"

I shook my head. The hard-and-fast rule at *The Journal-Times* was that an exclamation point was never to be used, unless it proclaimed the Second Coming—and then only with the editor's prior approval. Approval of the headline, that is; presumably, Jesus wouldn't need the editor's consent to show up.

I brought my parents up to date. They had heard a lot about Arch's death during their sojourn in Walnut Creek, of course, but were curious about the nitty-gritty details. When I told them about Billy Koenig's investigation techniques, Mom remarked, "Like London weather."

Dad lifted an eyebrow at me. Another of Mom's *non sequiturs.*

Mom caught our glance. "English weather forecasts often use 'intervals of brightness,' which reminds me of Chief Koenig."

"Your mother has such an interesting mind."

***

As we were clearing the lunch dishes, Sally appeared at the screen door, trundling a small cart with a bin of file folders and notebooks. She had called the day before and asked if she might stop by to go over plans for the Arts Festival. "Hi, Helen, Walter." She gave them each a hug. "Walter, so good to see you up and about."

I poured her a glass of sun tea and motioned her into the dining room where we had more room to spread out.

"Mom, Dad, why don't you join us? Maybe spot things that we missed."

"Well, if you don't mind, we'd like to hear more about the Heritage Week—and, of course, the Arts Festival," said Mom. She gestured with her hand at the room. "This was my parents' cottage, but not during the time I was growing up. They bought it when they retired. Meg often visited them in the summer and always came home with stories about the Fourth of July in Bramble."

"It's become quite an event," said Sally. "The Fourth of July is always combined with Heritage Week, and this year, the Arts Festival was added. Not to mention it's the last Independence Day of the twentieth century." Sally reached into her cart and pulled out a large calendar and a three-ring binder. She unfolded the calendar which showed the locations, and times of the Heritage Week events—all color-coded to spreadsheets and notes in the binder she placed on the table.

"Independence Day being next Sunday, it's the culmination of Heritage Week, which starts tonight, June thirtieth, with a formal dinner, with steak and lobster provided by The Heron, under a tent in the park near the beach."

Dad asked, "Are you going, Sally?"

"Craig and I bought tickets and would love to go, but it's going to be a long and busy week so we decided not to go."

"Same with Brad and me." I said.

Sally read from her book, "Tomorrow, Thursday, July first, is relatively quiet during the day—at least for most of Bramble. "We'll have our own one-day Taste of Bramble." She laughed. "I know, I know. It sounds like we're serving thorns and briars." She resumed. "There'll be long tables of food available on Main Street in front of Norton's, The Heron, and the Prairie Palace Hotel—everything from German potato salad and Polish sausages to Mexican enchiladas and nachos. Norton's will have ice cream and The Heron will serve tiny quiches. In the evening is Cruise Night on Main, with vintage automobiles and muscle cars on parade. Best of show, determined by the Classic Auto Club of Seminole County, receives a gift certificate for three free oil changes at Bert Schmidt's Garage."

Sally moved her finger to the Friday, July 2 square on the calendar. Consulting her book, she said, "At eight Friday morning is the 5K Bramble Ramble around Prairie Lake."

I added, "I remember one year I was here visiting Grandma and Grandpa Rasmussen, and some little boy won. All those men in their pricey jogging outfits, strutting around in T-shirts from other races they'd been in. Left behind in the dust."

"Several categories now, including a kids' category," laughed Sally, "so we avoid bruising delicate masculine egos. And all participants get a T-shirt. Also at eight in the morning is the judging of the shop window decorations. Thought it best to do it before the stores open and people kibbitz with the judges."

"The winner will be the Grand Marshal of the Fourth of July parade," I added.

"Who are the judges?" asked Mom.

I replied, "Well, we thought it best to select ones who will be as unbiased as possible, so the Chief of the Walnut Creek Fire Department, Pastor Joe, and Dr. Podolski will do the honors. We'll announce the winner at the Concert Under the Stars that same evening."

Sally turned the page in her notebook and ran her finger down it. "Where were we? Oh, yes. Saturday, July third. That's a busy day for us. Crafters and artists will set up at the Community Center—crafters in assigned spots in the parking lot, juried artists inside. While that's going on, Sandy Wilcox and her team from the church are supervising the canoe race, swimming races, parent-child softball game, and a beach volley ball tournament for teens."

"Canoe race, huh? I could take your canoe, Meg," Dad said hopefully.

"Hmm…you might want to rethink that idea, Dad," I said. "The winner is usually the last canoe still afloat. Everyone tries to capsize each other's canoes."

"Sounds rough," commented Mom.

"Definitely not for the faint of heart, but it sounds worse than it is. Canoeists help those in the water right their canoes and get to shore. All in good fun."

"After all that, what in the world is the Fourth itself like?" asked Dad. "What could possibly be left to do?"

"The Fourth being Sunday, Pastor Joe will hold a sunrise service on the shoreline in back of his church," I said. "Probably, the only sane part of the week.

"The parade steps off at nine o'clock and continues down Main Street and ends at the public beach for the flag raising and *National Anthem.* Horses, men riding tiny flying carpets, the Bramble High School marching band, clowns, Little League teams, cheerleaders, Boy Scouts, Girl Scouts, various clubs, floats." I laughed. "It's amazing there's anyone to watch the parade, because everyone is in it."

"Wow," said Mom. "Even floats."

"Well, it's not exactly the Rose Parade," replied Sally. "A float is any decorated vehicle with wheels—except for bicycles which are in a category of their own. Tractors, wheelbarrows, carts, kids' wagons, you name it."

"Don't forget the Bramble Irregulars," I said, "our very own kazoo band!"

"I'm exhausted just hearing about all this," said Mom.

I laughed. "And it isn't even time for the grand opening of the Community Center and Arts Festival at one o'clock Sunday afternoon!"

"Yes, that continues until five o'clock that evening when people can grab a bite to eat before they head down to the beach to get a spot to watch the fireworks over the lake," said Sally.

I added, "Boats watching from the lake itself are banned after one of the sailboats caught fire last July. No one was hurt but it was a bit like a Viking funeral."

Loud noises from Red Fox Lane interrupted us. I went over and opened the front door, looked out, and called over my shoulder to the others, "It's the trucks with the tent for tonight and other items for the week." I closed the door and came back inside.

"So glad that Frieda Koenig is handling the rest of Heritage Week," commented Sally. "The Arts Festival is more than enough for me."

"I hate to ask this," said Mom, "but is there something going on the next day? Most people have Monday off, too."

"Thank goodness, no!" responded Sally. "Frieda, Meg, and I signed up lots of people to help clean up and put the town back together. Work parties are scheduled for various areas—beach, Community Center, Main Street, et cetera, starting mid-morning on Monday—although the Arts Festival exhibitors will pack up on Sunday after the Arts Festival."

"You are a marvel, Sally," Mom said. "You're so organized."

"Thanks, but I have only a small part in all this. There are dozens and dozens of our neighbors who make the week happen." She reached over and touched my hand. "And of course, my friend, Meg, who fills in the gaps."

Chapter 26

Bright blue skies. Popcorn clouds. A light breeze caressing the lake with a soft kiss. Not quite. The day before Independence Day fell a bit short of idyllic. It was a typical hot and muggy Midwestern summer day and we wore the humidity like heavy garments. Nevertheless, we rejoiced; there was no rain predicted for the weekend.

Final touches on the Community Center continued unabated while Brambletonians enjoyed Heritage Week; workers from the landscaping company were finishing at the converted mansion while village workers marked off exhibitor display areas in the Center's parking lot area. Members of the Millennium Arts Committee were kept busy on site most of the week, helped by Sage Fletcher who was almost frenetic with activity. Last night, Brad and I took a break and attended the Concert Under the Stars. We both dozed on our blanket and left as soon as Norton's Betsy Ross was announced as the winner of the store window decoration contest—before the two of us added Snoring Under the Stars to the evening's entertainment.

Today, we walked over to Norton's for take-out coffees. Phil greeted us with a smile that nearly covered his entire face. "I suppose you heard the news," he said.

"We sure did, Phil. We were at the concert last night when the announcement was made. Congratulations on winning the store decoration prize!" Brad said. "Better exercise your arm for all that waving you're going to do as the Grand Marshal tomorrow!"

"Sage did all the work," said Phil. "I'm having her ride in the parade with me. I'm going to miss her when she starts school in a few weeks."

Carrying large coffees from Norton's carry-out bar, Brad and I headed over to the Community Center and greeted Sally, Craig, Martin Bryson, and Frieda Koenig. Already the parking lot pavement was hot underfoot. Sage Fletcher seemed to be everywhere, helping with signage and setting up displays. Frieda's sister-in-law, Gladys Koenig, brandishing a clip board and a folder bulging with copious notes, joined us a few minutes later and began haranguing Martin about the layout, waving a diagram under his nose. Craig sighed and said to us, "I'll handle this," and drew the two over to a shady spot on the edge of the parking lot.

Brad headed over to a picnic table where Gloria Morelli was sitting and fanning herself with an art show program under one of the huge maple trees that ringed the property. Her vibrant curls were hidden under an enormous straw hat. She would be handling the tickets for the Arts Festival, and Brad wanted to review the plans for making deposits until the bank opened on Tuesday.

Exhibitors began to arrive and Gladys was in officious heaven as she checked off their names, directed them to their display area, and went over the rules of the show. Most of the crafters were cottage industries, and their spouses, friends, and children lugged in bins and boxes. Pop-up tents and patio umbrellas sprang up as the parking area next to the Community Center was transformed into an outdoor bazaar filled with a colorful variety of items.

From a truck parked on the verge, three men from the rental company began to unload and set up the large white tent that had been used at Wednesday's formal dinner. It would be the food tent at the Community Center the next day. Max Trent hovered nearby, waiting to unload his truck filled with grills, tables, soft drinks, water, and other supplies. Frieda approved him to provide hot dogs and hamburgers, but at his regular prices, since this was a fund-raising event. The men wheeled a commercial refrigerator into the back of the tent. (Frieda had assured us that the huge appliance didn't come from the previous business at the site—Memory Gardens.)

Max and a couple of his employees began rolling aluminum ponies of beer down the ramp from the back of their truck toward the tent. It was soon evident they hadn't allowed for the pitch of the ramp and the slight downward slant of the parking lot. The kegs got away from them and began rolling toward the craft tables. The kegs gathered momentum and picked up speed. Some of the crafters scattered like ants in an overturned anthill, while others girded their loins (figuratively speaking) and stood bravely in the path of the runaway kegs. Finally, Max and his men caught up with the kegs and rolled them into the tent. Max gave a shout, "Guess we 'rolled out the barrel!'" The crafters laughed good-naturedly. As for Gladys Koenig, hers was not a pleasing countenance.

I walked over to Cam Podolski and Kim Winters as they got out of Cam's SUV parked along one side of the first-aid tent, and began unloading first-aid supplies, tables, a small cot, and other equipment.

"Hi! Can I be of any help?"

"Hi, Meg!" responded Kim. "I think Dr. Cam and I are okay, but thanks. We just came from the other first-aid station in the lifeguard shed at the lake. Nurses from the hospital are taking turns staffing it. So far, no one's suffered anything more than a few cuts and scrapes."

"That's good," I said. "We'll keep our fingers crossed it stays that way."

I walked over to the Community Center to check on the juried artists' work. As I came up, Sally was escorting the Winters twins, who were wheeling in the crates containing Arch Donegal's sculpture and Cyril Atkins' miniatures. All the while, Cyril Atkins trotted alongside, wringing his hands and mopping his brow. "Gently, gently. Please."

I followed them in and stopped for a moment to enjoy the air-conditioning. And the quiet—a calming change from the racket outside from cars, trucks, people shouting and hammering their booths together. Calm seemed to radiate from the interior of the Center with its paneling and soft lighting.

I remarked to Sally, "I almost feel bad. I mean, here's Arch Donegal dead with no one missing him, his lovely work on display, and what with all the Heritage Week goings-on, I haven't given him a thought for days."

In the large entry hall, I noticed to one side the stanchions and purple velvet ropes that the Winters boys had procured from the movie theater in Walnut Creek. Sally motioned the boys toward the large living room where various artwork was displayed. Many paintings and drawings were already in place. I was particularly struck by hand-made metal figures that seemed almost alive as they caught the sunlight streaming through the windows. I read the card next to them. George Cadotte! I had no idea our police sergeant was so talented.

"Sally, have you seen Celeste?" I asked. "I'm worried. It's not like her to be late—especially since she's a key player in the Arts Festival. I tried calling her, but there was no answer. I saw Gloria talking with Brad and asked her, but she had no idea she is."

Sally motioned me over to a corner of the room. "I am so sorry, Meg. With all the things going on to-day…well, I forgot to tell you that the Walnut Creek Wellness Center placed her on indefinite leave. At quite a bit less than full pay. She went to her office to pack up her things. She figured it would be pretty much empty today and she could avoid seeing anyone there, and having to explain. She said she might be late in arriving.”

Sally nodded. “And I know what you mean, Meg. But maybe it’s for the best to get our minds off murder for a little while, at least.”

“I’m for that. I wish I could.” Celeste had come up behind us.

A moment of awkward silence prevailed until Sally filled it by giving Celeste a hug. “Oh, Celeste, I have no words. So unfair of the Wellness Center.”

“I know you and the others are standing by me.” Giving a shrug of her shoulders, she said, “Let’s get busy.”

After delivering the miniatures to Cyril’s display area, the boys unpacked the crate holding the sculpture while Sally and I moved a small round table from a corner of the room to beneath the chandelier. Sally draped the table with a black velvet cloth that reached the floor. Todd and Tom picked up the statue and placed it as Sally indicated. She took the placard from the crate, put the card in a small frame, and turned on the chandelier. We were silent. The sculpture was breathtaking and shimmered in the light.

"Sure feels good in here. Nice and cool," came a voice from the doorway. Sage walked toward us and Sally turned to Celeste. "I don't think you've met our 'Jackie' of all trades. This is Sage Fletcher."

Celeste gave a start when Sally tapped her on the shoulder. "Sorry. Guess I'd drifted off. Too many things on my mind. I'm so glad to meet you at last, Sage. You've been such a valuable part of Heritage Week. Let me show you around the Center."

Sage gripped my arm. Her face was white and a sheen of perspiration began to bead on her forehead. As my mother would say, her eyes looked like two burnt holes in a blanket.

"Sage, come over here and sit down," I said, leading her to a chair.

"I'm okay," she said. "Really. Feel kinda chilled. Probably just dehydrated. I'll go over to the med tent, get some water, maybe sit for a bit." Sage tottered to the door.

"I'll go with you," I said, taking her arm.

"We'll both go," Celeste said.

Mercifully, the tent was open front and back, and the sides were rolled up a foot or two to catch what little breeze there was. Two large, rotating fans were moving the air. It was nowhere near as cool as inside the Center, but it was a relief to be away from the blistering sunlight. Kim came over, led Sage to a cot, filled a paper cup from the water cooler, and began wrapping her arm with a blood-pressure cuff.

Celeste said, "Kim, she's done so much for Heritage Week and the Festival. Is it okay if I pop in and keep her company for a while?"

"Sure. If you can stay with her just a bit, I need to run over to the Center and use their facilities," Kim said. "Trying to avoid using the Porta-Potties." She grimaced.

I lifted the tent flap and motioned Celeste inside. I glanced at Celeste, who remained motionless at my side. She seemed lost in thought.

"Celeste?" I prompted.

She started. "Oh, Meg, I'm sorry…the heat must be getting to me, too." She smiled and asked, "How are you feeling, Sage?"

"I think I'm a bit better. I'm really sorry not to be able to work today."

"Sage, you've done wonderful things to help make the Festival a success. We are all so grateful. Couldn't have done it without you." She sat on the lawn chair next to the cot. "Tell me about yourself. Meg says you're going to start school at Chicago Art Institute…"

As Kim and I left the tent, we narrowly missed colliding with Wallace Arnhart, who was carrying a sheaf of papers and a small bag. "Hi, er, Wally," I said and nodded at the things he carried. "What's up?"

"Putting up campaign posters. Everyone who is anyone will be here," he smirked. "Even women." He stepped inside the tent and rummaged around in his bag until he found a roll of tape.

"Oh, no, you don't, Wallace," said Kim. "This is a medical tent, not a campaign platform."

"It's a public event."

"And this tent belongs to me. Your posters are not going in here."

Two or three exhibitors had stopped to listen to the discussion. Arnhart picked up his materials. "Typical woman. Standing in the way of progress." He swaggered off.

The exhibitors exchanged glances and one said to Kim, "You go, girl!"

"That man!" said Kim. "Our patients would relapse if they had to look at his poster while they were in here."

"He's a piece of work, that's for sure," I said.

I left them chatting and went over to the Community Center. Celeste came in a few minutes later. She stopped inside and gazed for a long minute at the bronze shining under the chandelier. She turned on her heel and walked over to help with one of the other art displays.

Sally followed her to lend a hand and I went outside to see if I could help any of the crafters with theirs. The Art Festival's outdoor craft show was taking shape, and boasted a variety of homemade items: jewelry, essential oils, wooden birdhouses, homemade soap, barrettes (does anyone over the age of six wear these?), doilies and antimacassars, spices. And no sweet little boxes made with tongue depressors.

The crafters all were helping one another and I spotted a man in a T-shirt bearing the words, "For the Birds," putting a canvas awning over the table he shared with some needlecrafters. As I admired an exquisite framed cross-stitch of an angel, donated by Sally, Mom stood up from where she'd crouched as she reached under the table for a box.

"Yikes, Mom! You startled me," I said.

"Hi, Meg." From the box she pulled Dad's teapot and Aunt Gae's cozy and set them out with a placard marked "sold."

"Wow! Did someone buy the teapot and cozy?"

Mom laughed. "Oh, no." She winked at me. "I would never sell Gae's cozy when you've found so many uses for it. Or the teapot your dad made. I marked the pair as sold so none of the other crafters would sell them. We're all helping each other with sales so we can take a break now and then."

I was about to turn away when Gladys Koenig strode over, plunked a large box down on the table with a thud that shook the table, and said with self-importance, "This is *my* table."

"Actually, according to the program" said Mom, "It's *our* table." She pulled a program from her box and pointed to a diagram of the exhibit booths.

"Well!" huffed Gladys. "I don't know how *that* happened. I see Celeste Farnsworth's fine hand in this." She sneered and muttered something under her breath. "I guess it'll have to do." She looked at the two items on the table. "There should be enough room for my things if you squeeze over a bit."

Mom moved Sally's needlework and the teapot a fraction of an inch as Gladys arranged several of her creations—afghans in a rainbow of colors (if rainbows were neon, which, thankfully, they are not).

I exchanged eyerolls with the "birdhouse man." Knowing there are others whose eyeballs are, um, expressive, gave me a glow of delight. Well, not really—the temperature was way too high to add anything warm—even a glow—to it.

I motioned to the bottles of water in a cooler near the table. "Good you're staying hydrated. It's a scorcher today," I said.

"Yes," Mom replied. "I heard Sage became ill. Hope she's okay. She's been so helpful. Young people don't always realize they're susceptible to the effects of hot weather. I heard Phil Norton won the store decoration contest and is going to have her ride with him in the parade tomorrow."

"Yes. Brad and I were at the concert last night when the announcement of the Grand Marshal was made. We saw Phil this morning. He is over the moon! We were a little surprised Sage's *Washington Crossing the Delaware* on Bushel O'Bargains' window didn't win, although her Betsy Ross was very good, too."

Mom leaned forward and said, conspiratorially, "My sources tell me that Wallace wiped off most of the picture, completely ruined it."

I laughed. "Your sources?"

"You would be amazed at how much these craft people know! And tell!"

"Sounds like he found Frieda's campaign slogan hidden on the hull of Washington's boat."

"Yes. I imagine so." Mom frowned. "Poor Sage. I wouldn't want that man as an enemy."

I ambled over to the table filled with birdhouses. Detail and craftsmanship coupled with clever ideas convinced me I had to have one. I selected a yellow one which Ron "For the Birds" told me was just right for wrens, and had him set it aside until I had my purse with me.

I noticed that the library's pop-up booth was in place, with books still in plastic bins to protect them in case it rained overnight. Tomorrow there would be a book sale and a story time for kids to enjoy having books read to them. And snacks and juice, of course, while their parents looked around the exhibits.

The heat of the day was unrelenting. I walked over to Kim Winters who was standing just inside the medical tent. "Come in out of the sun, Meg, and sit down. Your arms are starting to look lobster-y. I'll get you some water."

I took off my sunglasses and looked down at my arms. They had that pink blotchy forerunner of sunburn.

Kim returned and handed me a bottle of water. "Here you go." She also handed me a tube of sunblock. "Better late than never."

After a long drink, I set the bottle down and began smearing the lotion on my forearms.

"Get your neck and face, too, Meg. You're red all around where your sunglasses were." She held up a small mirror. My eyes were circled in white. I looked like a pink raccoon.

I glanced over at the cot where Sage was sleeping. "How is she, Kim?"

"That girl was exhausted. I'm glad she's getting some rest."

"Kim, please let me know when she's ready to go home. I'll go with her, get her settled."

"Oh, that would be great, Meg."

As I started back to the Center, a truck bearing the slogan, "Search No More for the Wright Solution," drove in to the area roped off for unloading materials. Gabe Wright and two other men in work clothes opened the back, and began to take out tarps to cover the outdoor booths overnight. I quickened my step before Wright saw me. Odious man.

***

Twilight was yielding to a soft darkness as Sally, Craig, and I closed up the Community Center and locked the doors. The temporary lights strung around the parking lot were already on. Brad and I had agreed to meet at my house after he accompanied Gloria Morelli to the bank's night depository. I said goodnight to Craig and Sally and went over to the med tent to pick up Sage.

On the way, I noticed one of Gabe's men lounging against one of the booths and smoking a cigarette. Good thing Frieda isn't here to see him. He'd never survive a tongue-lashing by Fred Koenig's sweetie pie. As I got closer, I recognized him as the security guard at the reception desk at the coroner's office. "Hi, Frank!" I said.

"Um…" I could tell he had no idea who I was.

"I met you at the Seminole County building."

"Oh, yeah."

Sage and Kim Winters were standing outside the tent as I approached. Kim was yawning, her hands on the small of her back, stretching as I approached.

"Sorry, Meg. It's been a long day. Dr. Podolski was tired when he arrived, what with their new baby and all, so I made him go home a couple of hours ago. Even though we'll have a lot of people coming here tomorrow, most of them won't be hitting their thumbs with hammers or straining their backs carrying things into the booths. And we have water stations scattered around."

I turned to Sage. "How are you feeling, Sage? You gave us quite a scare this morning."

Sage scuffed her toe in the ground. "I'm really sorry about that. I guess I overdid it." She looked at me. "You really don't have to do this, Meg. Like, I just live across the street over the hardware store."

"Just want to make sure you're okay."

Sage shrugged and the two of us left the parking lot and walked over to Ben's Hardware. She pulled out her key and the two of us stepped inside. The security lights were on and in the dimness I looked around. Next to book stores, I loved being in hardware stores best. And Ben's was a delight with its vintage signs, the wooden counter where Ben tallied up customer purchases on butcher paper, and the pulley system leading to the loft where Ben's wife, Nina, made change. Tonight, evidence of the busy days prior to Heritage Week was scattered over the counter.

"Sorry about the mess," Sage said. "I haven't had a chance to clean up everything we used for wrapping purchases and stuff. That's one of my jobs in return for my free room. Shop is closed tomorrow, so I can get at it then." She motioned toward the stairway at one side of the store. "Guess I'll be off. Thank you, Meg."

"I'll go upstairs with you."

"No. No, I'm fine."

"Okay, but hop right into bed, Sage. You have to be well enough to ride at the head of the parade with Phil Norton tomorrow."

"Yeah, Betsy Ross won."

As I walked home, I gazed at the magnificent and humbling panoply of stars. Instead of the serenity I usually experienced by losing myself in the night skies, I felt a disquietude. Something about the day eluded me. Something important I missed. The image of the witches in *Macbeth* stirring their cauldron flashed through my mind. I laughed softly. Next I'll be cackling and making predictions by the pricking of my thumbs.

Chapter 27

The Fourth had arrived. Pastor Joe caught up with me as I passed his church on my way to the parade on Main Street. I love parades, especially the unsophisticated Bramble event. No fancy floats made possible by the sacrifice of thousands of flowers, no giant balloon figures hovering grotesquely overhead, no running commentary by announcers speaking in voices of practiced enthusiasm.

"Hi, Meg!" he said. "Another scorcher coming up today. I'm glad the back of the church faces north. It was already pretty warm at the sunrise service today. Still, we had a good turn-out." He made no comment about my absence from said service and walked along companionably with me. He wore a large straw hat and was dressed in civvies, that is, an open-necked, short-sleeved shirt and no clerical collar.

"You go on, Pastor Joe," I said. "I want to check on something."

I went over to the lead vehicle—the red Cadillac convertible made famous at the mayoral debate, Frieda Koenig, and to a lesser degree, her driver and campaign manager. Phil Norton was standing beside it.

"Where's Sage?" I asked. "Is she okay? I thought she was going to ride with you."

"I haven't seen her and I can't leave the car and go over to her place. It's not like her to not show up. We're going to start pretty soon."

"Uh-oh. I'd better check on her. She was sick yesterday." Seeing Phil's worried face, I added, "Go ahead and start the parade without her if you need to."

Phil started to protest, then nodded. "You're right, Meg. No point holding up everyone else."

I half-ran, half-walked to Ben's Hardware—skirting several families lugging blankets and lawn chairs to watch the parade on Main Street. When I arrived at the store, the door was locked, so I rang the doorbell Ben had installed for Sage's little apartment upstairs. Ben and Nina Fulton had left early for the Art Festival—Ben to help with any last-minute carpentry, Nina to assist Gloria Morelli with handling the sales. I was about to ring again when Sage came to the door. Her face was bone-white, her hair askew, and she hugged a blanket she had wrapped around her.

"Sage! Are you okay?"

"Yeah. I guess Ben and Nina let me sleep in." She gave a start. "Meg! I'm supposed to ride in the parade with Phil." Her words came out in a rush. "And I have to help with the fair…make sure the tents tables statue artists tickets…"

"Oh, no, you don't! You take your blanket and get right on upstairs. Do you have enough water? Something to eat?"

"Yeah, but I…" She staggered a bit as she took a few steps.

I helped her upstairs and got her settled. "Sage, you stay in bed today. I'll send one of the nurses back to check on you. You're sure you're okay for food and water?"

"I'll be okay," Sage said. Her eyes were already half-closed. I closed the door softly, went downstairs, and left the building.

I scurried along the sidewalk to where Pastor Joe was in front of Johnny's Bait Emporium, the building providing a bit of shade. Johnny McTavish had moved to Tennessee but one of his relatives had opened the shop for the summer, prior to putting it up for sale. Some of the Bramble kids had decorated his shop windows with a drawing of a fat fish about to savor a plump red, white, and blue worm grimacing in terror as it dangled from a fishing line.

Both sides of the street were lined with people. Small children in strollers and small children who should be in strollers. Many families came early, with several lawn chairs to stake out their claims on choice viewing spots. It reminded me of my years in Chicago when it snowed and neighborhood residents secured parking spots with chairs.

The Community Center was roped off until it opened after lunch. Gabe Wright's security men, their arms crossed in front of them in that way men do to make their biceps look bigger, stood in front of the entrance. Outside in the Center's parking lot, craft fair exhibitors were chatting with one another as they fussed with their booths.

And here came the parade, led by Phil Norton, waving and tipping his straw boater to the crowds. Children. Dogs. More decorated bicycles than I could count. Several riding lawn mowers and one wheelbarrow festooned with streamers.

Pastor Joe waved and shouted as a wagon advertising that year's Vacation Bible School rolled by, filled with screaming Sunday School children, their voices shrill with excitement. The air was soon filled with small missiles as the kids hurled candy at the onlookers. The parade was moving slowly, so Pastor Joe walked over to the wagon and reminded the kids to use an underhand toss instead of imitating Roger Clemens.

A white convertible bearing Freddy Squared glided by—Hizzoner in his glory and waving while Frieda looked as if her toenails were being pulled out one by one.

Following the Girl Scout troop was a baby-blue Jeep driven by Hattie Perkins, owner of the dry cleaning and tailor shop. She was dressed as Douglas Macarthur, complete with aviator sunglasses, while a trio of women dressed as the Andrews Sisters sang songs from the 1940s from the back seat.

A color guard of Cub Scouts. Little girls in pink, twirling and dropping small batons. The obligatory Medinah Shriners, their flying carpets belching fumes as they wove in and out. An antique Ford with this year's Miss Bramble, a pretty Black senior at Bramble High School, waving from the rumble seat. Ella Chapin in an abbreviated silver lamé drum majorette outfit, her "big hair" held in place with enough hairspray to create its own hole in the ozone, marking time for the Bramble kazoo band with her aluminum foil-wrapped plumbing plunger. A man in lederhosen playing German folk songs on a glockenspiel. Several marching bands creating a joyful, if jumbled, noise.

As soon as the parade and the last of the yapping dogs that ran alongside passed by, I walked over to the Community Center. I hated to miss the flag-raising, as the Andrews Sisters were to sing the *National Anthem,* but the day ahead promised to be a busy one. And I had to watch for Kim Winters so when she arrived, I could ask her to check in on Sage.

I ducked under the rope and walked toward the Community Center building. The front door was open and I could sense a crisis of some sort. I squeezed past Gabe Wright and joined Sally and Celeste who were standing under the chandelier. The velvet-draped table was overturned and Arch Donegal's bronze was on the floor.

***

I stood, aghast. "What happened?"

Celeste said, "When Sally and I opened up this morning, we found it like this."

"I'll pick the metal thing up and put it over there on the couch," said Gabe.

"You will not touch it, Mr. Wright!" snapped Frieda Koenig who had entered right behind me. "You were supposed to be providing security so something like this wouldn't happen."

"I had men patrolling all night," said Wright, a whine slipping into his voice. "We're not responsible for inside the building. One of youse left the door unlocked."

Everyone talked at once until Sally clapped her hands and shouted, "Enough!" The group was silent. "The Arts Festival will open in a couple of hours. Let's first do something about this…this…" She took a deep breath. "Celeste, would you please examine the bronze and see if there's any damage? Everyone else, let's go over to the conversation area and sit down."

Celeste knelt on the floor and studied the statue in the light provided by the sunlight streaming through the open door. "Meg, can you help turn this over? It's really heavy."

Together we turned the statue over. I stood out of her way while Celeste continued her scrutiny. Finally, she stood up. "There doesn't seem to be any damage, thank God. The thickness of the carpeting prevented it."

Just then, Martin Bryson came in. He stared, horrified, at the bust on the floor. "What…?" He righted the table. "It's too wobbly," he said. "Leg's broken, won't hold that lovely work."

We found another table and draped it. The drape didn't quite reach the floor, but none of us cared at that point. Celeste reached out to help Martin lift the bust. "I can manage. Not to worry," he said. But his hands shook as he placed it gently on the table.

"Uh-oh," I said. "The description card is gone."

"I have something that might work." Martin pulled a business card from his wallet and hand-lettered the description on the back. It would have to do. The Art Fair was upon us.

Chapter 28

A line to enter the Community Center grounds had already formed on the sidewalk. The chatter as people wandered through the craft tables was heartening after the morning's near-disaster. Minutes later, Brad opened the Community Center doors and visitors began coming in. Gloria sat inside the door where those buying a piece of art would pay. To avoid depleting the fine arts displays, they were issued a receipt and would return after the show closed and pick up their purchase.

Sage took no more convincing to stay in her apartment, but her energy and enthusiasm were missed. She had signed up to read to children at the library's booth. Millie Pullen volunteered to fill in and Sally reluctantly agreed. As Sally and I walked by the booth later, we were amazed at Millie's animated style and her ability to imitate various characters' voices. The kids loved it. Sally and I looked at each other and mouthed, "Who knew?"

I heard several people ask Cyril Atkins if his "doll houses" were for sale. To his credit, he calmly corrected them and said they were for display only. He handed out brochures detailing how the miniatures were made.

The afternoon went faster than I imagined it would. We saw nearly every villager as they came in to look at the art and, guided by docents that Sally had appointed and trained, took tours of the completed downstairs of the Center. The stairs and elevator were roped off. About half-way through the afternoon, Jon Dreher and Louis Briggs came through the back door with refreshments and snacks. I helped them pass them out to the artists and workers.

"Wow!" exclaimed Jon as the two walked over to where George Cadotte was standing at the table with his metal art work.

"Sergeant, I had no idea," said Louis. "You've been moonlighting."

Cadotte laughed. "Please call me George. I'm definitely off duty today."

"Jon, let's get this one," said Louis, indicating the figure of a horse and rider. "It would look marvel-ous in our den."

"Absolutely!" his partner agreed.

George gave them the card with title and price of the piece they'd selected and replaced it with a hand-lettered "Sold" sign. I was delighted to see that several of his works had been purchased already.

***

A few minutes before closing time, with only a few visitors remaining, the crafters were starting to pack up their unsold merchandise, and those who bought fine art were arriving to collect their purchases. About a half-hour later, the crafters were gone, the last of the art buyers had left, and the artists began putting boxes and bins containing their unsold pieces on carts to take to their vehicles. The parking lot was nearly empty. Brad came inside where he met Cyril Atkins, and the two of them began placing Atkins' delicate miniatures in their custom-made shipping containers.

Pete Winters arrived with Tom and Todd, and the three hoisted the stanchions and ropes into the back to take back to the Walnut Creek theater. The three of them came back inside, lifted *Carina* from the table, wrapped it in blankets, and carried it to Pete's truck. The miniatures were next.

Cyril was horrified when he realized his precious works were to be transported in the Pump N

Dump truck. Pete assured him that the truck was used only for managing his business, not for pumping or dumping septic tanks. Nonetheless, Cyril insisted on examining the truck minutely before committing his art work to the short ride to the library.

Everything secured in the truck and Cyril satisfied that no indication of the business's purpose was present, Sally left with them to unlock the library where the pieces would be kept in her office until shipped from there on Tuesday.

*****

I'd invited the Sally and Craig over to watch the fireworks from my house that evening. When they begged off, citing near-exhaustion, I made not even a token protest. I was beat too. A long shower, jammies, and the carry-out dinners supplied to us by Louis and Jon were about all I could manage. Brad, my parents, and I watched the fireworks, which were more elaborate and longer than usual, marking the last Fourth of July of the twentieth century. The display finally ended with a huge American flag blazing and crackling overhead, and we dragged ourselves inside.

Chapter 29

When I arrived at the Community Center the next morning, Frieda Koenig and Sally were there surveying the cleanup work. The village street cleaners had finished their work. Other than ourselves and a few young people sweeping up debris into large garbage bags, not another person was in sight. A sleek orange cat trotted across the street as if on a mission and disappeared behind one of the buildings. Even though the store decorations were still in place, the shops were closed and Main Street was leached of life, the excitement of Heritage Week dissipated. Even the youngsters talked in hushed voices. The town of Bramble was returning to its customary languor. I could almost sense its relief.

***

One afternoon a few days later, Sally called to suggest that the two of us get together to go over the events of the Arts Festival. She'd scheduled a wrap-up meeting of MAC for next week and Sally, being Sally, wanted to get a head start.

Mom and Dad had gone to lunch with some new friends they made at the craft fair, so I offered my kitchen table and a jug of sun tea. Sally brought her to-die-for lemon cookies which we munched as we talked. The Arts Festival had done well financially, and the income would go a long way toward finishing the main building. At length, Sally gathered up the papers except for a yellow legal pad. A pencil poised in her hand, she said, "I think we need to try to figure who and why someone toppled over the statue. I mentioned it in my report, as you know, but the whole incident troubles me."

"Me too, Sally." I paused. "Not just that, but all the other episodes that have happened in our town."

"In that case, let's not limit ourselves."

"How do you mean?"

Sally drew the pad closer. "Let's make a list of all the incidents and see if we can make some progress toward sorting things out."

I felt the investigative reporter stir within me. "Let's!"

"Okay," Sally said. She drew four columns on the paper. "There! Incident, means, motive, opportunity. Let's get the robbery at Bushel O'Bargains out of the way first. It wasn't really a robbery since there was only damage—broken bottles, stuff pulled off the shelves, and the like—no cash or liquor taken. And, of course, the beating they gave Wally Arnhart—cuts, lots of bruises, and a real shiner." She poised her pencil over the yellow pad. "It happened after closing hours, right?"

"Yes. I looked at the lock and the door. No damage. He must've let the guys in. Or he opened the door and they forced their way in. There wasn't enough damage done by the intruders to merit much of an insurance claim." I thought for a moment. "We don't know much about Wallace, come to think of it. He and his store have always just been here."

I refilled our glasses and we sat in silence for a few minutes. We didn't come up with any more ideas, so Sally wrote "Break-in Motive" in her notes.

"As long as we're on the subject of break-ins," said Sally, "let's look at the episode with Arch's statue at the Arts Festival."

I sighed. She caught my look of impatience cross my face. "I know, I know. I want to discuss Arch's murder too, but that's going to take us a while, and I'd really like to brainstorm ideas about who tried to damage the display. See if we come up with something before the MAC wrap-up meeting."

I acquiesced. She did have a point.

"First of all," I began, "Why was only Arch's work targeted? The other artists' displays were already set up but were untouched."

"Oh, Meg, I hadn't thought of that," Sally replied. "If it had been mischief or vandalism, I would've thought other pieces would've been meddled with." She made a note. "It would've been a disaster. I can't imagine how we would've managed. So many valuable pieces. Can you imagine the uproar? Especially from Cyril Atkins if his miniatures had been damaged?"

"Speaking of Atkins," I said, "something occurred to me after we'd unpacked his miniatures that day in your office. Why were his doll houses (I permitted myself an eye roll as I used the term), shipped to us from the UK?"

"What do you mean? That's where he's from."

"Well, he said Bramble was his third stop, he'd already displayed his work in Michigan and Wisconsin. Surely, he would use the same miniatures at each location, especially since his brochure features them. So why didn't he ship them directly from Door County to Bramble?"

Sally and I couldn't come up with a logical explanation, so Sally made another note, and we picked up our discussion of Arch's statue. I said, "Frieda reported it to the police at the time and told them about the missing display card."

"There's been no action that I know of. Billy Koenig is a good man, but only tectonic plates move more slowly."

"Who had keys to the Community Center?" I asked. "There wasn't any evidence of forced entry."

"And," added Sally, "before we locked up, we went around and checked all the rooms and closets—upstairs and down—to make sure everything was tidy for the festival the next day. So no one was lurking inside overnight."

She continued. "Keys," she wrote on her legal pad as she talked. "You, me, and Celeste have keys. Oh, and Frieda, of course. We gave one to the police department. And I imagine Martin Bryson has Arch's key."

"I don't think so. Arch would've had his key with him when he died, and, as far as I know, all of his effects on his body are still in the evidence room at the police station. Before you ask, the evidence room is surprisingly secure. I was there the other day."

"Oh, that's right. We had to have the hardware store make another key for Martin."

"What about Gabe Wright and his security guys? Frank Makar?"

Sally's mouth curled in a moue of disgust. "Before work began on the Community Center, Wright presented a bid to the village board to provide security at the work site. But the board horsed around, wanting to save the village money and have the police patrol the site instead. And, I have to say that Chief Koenig's men did a fine job. But I had to agree with Frieda that our police force would be too stretched to cover Heritage Week this year. I've thought all along that there's something nasty about Gabe Wright. Thank goodness we didn't give him a key or ask him to patrol inside the building. I wouldn't trust him any farther than I could throw him." She made another note on her pad.

"Horsed around! That's it! Wright's security guy, Frank Makar! He was working at the reception desk at the Seminole County building when I went to talk with Jim Dowd."

"What? Slow down, Meg. I'm not following you."

"It was before Gabe Wright made his presentation to MAC, so I didn't recognize the Wright logo on Makar's shirt. Makar was talking on the phone with someone when I came in and I heard part of the conversation, something about five to one, so I thought he was making an appointment. There was a document in front of him, but he covered it up with his arm when I came up to the desk. A few minutes later, when he answered another phone call, I snuck a look at it. I saw only the number 8, followed by the letters AQUE, and didn't figure it out until now. Aqueduct!"

Sally frowned. "I'm still not following you."

"Aqueduct! The New York racetrack! Makar was poring over a racing form for Race Number 8 that day at Aqueduct! And 'five to one' wasn't an appointment time—Makar was quoting odds on a bet over the phone! So it looks like this Frank Makar guy and maybe even Gabe Wright, himself, are involved in gambling."

Sally added, "And it was Arch Donegal, addicted to gambling, who recommended Wright's company!"

She jotted down a lengthy entry. At this rate, she'd soon have enough material to publish a book.

"There!" she said, laying her pencil on the table. She leaned back in her chair, linked her fingers together in front of her, and stretched. Outside, the room brightened by the midday sun earlier had faded to the soft buff of late afternoon. Minerva came into the kitchen, crouched by her food bowl, and stared unblinking at me.

Sally glanced at her watch. "I've got to go. Craig will wonder what happened to me."

"Shall we meet here again tomorrow? Maybe mid-morning so we'll have more time to talk about Arch's murder?"

"Sounds great," Sally said. "I'll bring lunch. I have a couple of casseroles in my freezer."

Of course she did.

***

Shortly after Sally left, Mom and Dad returned from their outing—with Jon and Louis following on their heels and bearing food.

"We figured you wouldn't have time to cook, Meg, after spending most of the afternoon with Sally, so we thought we'd drop off some goodies," said Louis, giving me a peck on the cheek after setting down several covered dishes.

Jon grinned. "Meg? Cooking? I think he meant you, Mrs. Smyth. Meg told us you and your husband were out gallivanting with some new friends."

"Guys," replied Dad, "please just call us Helen and Walter."

"Yes, please do," agreed Mom. "When you say, 'Mrs. Smyth,' I think of my mother-in-law." Mom paused, then followed with flurry of words praising the positive attributes of my Grandmother Smyth. A surprised look crossed Dad's face. Privately, Mom and Dad referred to his mother as Brünnhilde.

"That's a lot of food," I said. "And it smells divine. Thanks so much."

"Yes, thank you," said Mom. "Can you two stay for a bit?"

"No, thanks. We're on the way to The Heron," said Jon. "Evening shift's beginning soon."

After enjoying the sumptuous meal, Dad settled himself in front of the television while Mom and I tidied up the kitchen. "So, Mom, what did you do all day?"

"Well, Stan and Gert live in Restful Ponds…"

"Oh?" I responded as nonchalantly as possible.

"I know what I've said about mobile home, but I have to say theirs is much nicer than I imagined. So peaceful, lots of trees. There's a couple of units for sale and we walked through them."

"Mm-hmm."

"Anyway, we had sandwiches for lunch on their deck and spent the day chatting about this and that. Did you and Sally uncover anything more about all these goings-on in Bramble?"

I told her about the possibility of organized gambling in Bramble run by Gabe Wright.

"The security guy? That's awful. People trust them and…" Mom yawned, stood up, and hugged me. "I want to hear more, but all that fresh air today is getting to me. I'll give your father a nudge—I'm sure he's snoozing in front of the TV as usual—and go on up to bed."

***

It was still early and I was restless. I prowled around downstairs, straightening a couple of throw rugs, using my foot to nudge a lamp cord under a table, picking up the TV remote and putting it down again, until I was ready to give up and open my laptop and check emails for Miss Polly. As I entered the kitchen, I saw Brad at the back door.

"Am I glad to see you! You saved me—or, rather, you saved Miss Polly." I nodded toward my computer.

"Always glad to save a damsel in distress." He bent and kissed me. "What is that wonderful smell?"

"Jon and Louis dropped off dinner. There's a bit left. I didn't save much for you because you said you were clearing out the debris left from your construction at your house, getting the dumpster filled tonight."

"Never got around to working on the house, but not to worry—I'm not hungry. Had dinner with Cyril Atkins tonight. I'll just grab a beer from your refrigerator." Brad sat down and popped the cap off the bottle.

"Cyril Atkins? How did that come about?"

"We got to know each other a bit at the Arts Festival and he's still in town, so I bought him dinner at the hotel." Brad took a swig from the bottle. "So how did things go today with the vigil-aunties?"

I replied archly, "If, perchance, by that you mean Sally and me, we discovered—actually, deduced—a lot about..." I paused for dramatic effect. "Gambling!"

I went over with Brad my experience with Frank Makar at the county office and the connection between Arch Donegal and the security company.

"I'm sorry to hear that you've learned so much."

"What! Sorry? Why?"

He sighed. "I guess I'm going to have to fill you in on what's happening. I know you'll keep plugging at it, and I don't want you to get hurt. The people involved are dangerous." Brad looked into my eyes. "What I'm about to tell you is strictly confidential. You can't even tell Sally. The situation will be resolved by the end of tomorrow."

"You have my word, Brad. I don't want to endanger whatever the plan is or anyone involved in it— especially you. Be careful. Gabe Wright is unsavory, to say the least. And his henchman, Frank Makar, even looks like a thug."

Brad nearly choked on his beer.

"What?"

Brad gasped, "Frank Makar. Thug."

My annoyance was growing. "What about him?"

"He's an FBI special agent."

I stared, open-mouthed. "And you've been involved in this all along?"

"No, I learned of it just this evening. As a courtesy, really, since I'll be retiring soon."

"I thought you had dinner with Atkins."

"I did."

"Don't tell me he's an FBI agent too?"

Brad laughed. "Dear God, no! I can't imagine that prissy little man…J. Edgar would…" Brad took a swig of his beer.

"You should know that the Sally and I discussed how odd it was that Atkins had his miniatures shipped from the UK, instead of from Door County where he had exhibited them last."

"He came directly here from England," Brad said. "The U.S. stops were a cover story."

"But he really is a miniaturist?"

"Oh, yes. That part is true. But it would seem odd if he came all the way from London to the little town of Bramble, to an unknown Arts Festival."

"The whole thing seems odd, Brad. What *is* he doing in Bramble?"

"He represents the Masters of Wine."

"Wallace Arnhart!" I shouted. Minerva skittered to the safety of the windowsill. I lowered my voice, belatedly remembering my parents sleeping upstairs.

"What do you know about Arnhart—other than he'd make a terrible mayor?" Brad asked.

"I really don't know him at all. But as far as Cyril Atkins, it just seemed odd that he pitched right in and helped Sage and me clean up Bushel O'Bargains after the break-in the night before."

"Well," said Brad, "it seems Wallace Arnhart has been counterfeiting wine labels. Placing fake high-end wine labels on bottles of lower quality wines. We had someone bag up the broken bottles—some of them with phony labels—from the shop's garbage cans in the alley."

"Oh no. Please tell me that Sage isn't doing the artwork for it."

"Not to worry. This was going on long before she arrived."

I thought for a bit. "This is a lot to take in," I said. "Do you think the gambling and the counterfeit wine labels are related?"

"In a way," Brad answered. "Arnhart was laundering the gambling money for Wright and using the kickback he received to run his label business. They must've had a falling-out over something, which is why Arnhart was beaten up over it."

"You said all this would resolved tomorrow, right?"

"Arrest warrants are being finalized and…" Brad stopped and shook his head. "I suppose there's no way to keep you from reporting this."

"You suppose right."

"Okay, We'll need to work something out so it looks like you just happened on the scene."

"The press never sleeps!"

"Hmm," he said, the corners of his mouth quirking up. "What a tantalizing thought."

Chapter 30

Because I knew about it in advance, the arrests early next morning at Bushel O'Bargains were almost anticlimactic. But it gave me time to get my trusty Nikon from the closet to snap a few photos for *The Journal-Times*. I was removing the lens cover when Danny Muir, the latest bright young thing interning at the *Bramble Buzz* came running up, his lank brown hair hanging in his eyes. "Hi, Meg!" He wiped his forehead on his shirt sleeve. "What's going on? Wow! Must be a biggie with the paddy wagon from Walnut Creek here."

"Patrol wagon." I automatically corrected the derogatory term originally referring to the large number of Irish users of the vehicle—both policemen and passengers—in New York in the early 1900s. The term was still in the vernacular, but prohibited by reputable newspapers. Danny had already dashed over to Chief Koenig and missed my educational message.

Koenig shooed Danny away like a pesky fly. When the Chief saw my camera, however, he beckoned me over. Danny was so crestfallen that I nodded for him to come along but motioned him to stay behind me, out of the way.

As we watched, Sergeant Cadotte escorted a cuffed Wallace Arnhart from the store. He dipped his head, but not before I snapped a couple of photos as he climbed into the back of the police vehicle. The door of the shop opened again, and Chip Kelly emerged with Frank Makar, also hand-cuffed. Evidently, Makar was still undercover so I took a photo or two of him as he joined Arnhart in the vehicle.

Keeping my pledge to Brad not to reveal my prior knowledge of the arrests, I scribbled notes as I talked with Koenig, who was so puffed up, I feared he might explode. "Really big. This is really big," he said, in a voice sounding like Ed Sullivan. "Will really put Bramble on the map."

"On the map?" I queried. Surely another crime wasn't part of the marketing strategy for the village.

"Um, I mean for insightful police work," he said.

"Of course."

He went on to tell me about the gambling ring and the wine label counterfeiting as I nodded and took notes, giving him an occasional feigned look of amazement.

"Are there any other people implicated?" I asked.

"Well, little lady," he said, patting my arm. "That's for me to know and you to find out." He turned and walked toward his squad car before I could reply.

"Wow!" said Danny Muir, whom I'd forgotten was behind me. "That was great. Your questions were terrific. Of course, you've been a journalist for a really long time."

He jogged off to *The Buzz* office before I could regale him with my fondness for stegosaurus burgers and other joys of my long-ago youth. I shook my head and tottered off toward home.

***

Not long afterward, Sally arrived with a picnic basket, complete with red gingham cloth, from which she began pulling various luncheon items, including a yellow enameled casserole dish. "I'll pop this in the oven to warm it up when we're ready to eat," she said.

"Go ahead now, if you're hungry," I replied. "I've had an exciting morning."

The oven set and the casserole warming, Sally said, "Tell me."

"We were right! There has been a gambling operation going on! The police arrested Wally Arnhart and that, um, Frank Makar guy this morning!"

"Are we good or what?!"

"Brad calls us the vigil-aunties."

"I'm not sure that's a compliment, but I'll take it," Sally said.

"But wait! There's more!"

"You sound like that carpet salesman who's on television."

"Wally has been laundering money for the gambling operation and putting counterfeit labels on some of his wine."

"You're kidding, Meg. How did they find out about that? There aren't many wine 'noses' around here to discover the switch."

"There is one wine connoisseur in town, Sally."

She looked blank. Then I almost could see a light bulb go on over her head. "Cyril Atkins!"

"Yep. His wine club or whatever sent him over here."

"So he's, what? An Interpol agent?"

"I don't know, but he's going to be a witness, I'm sure."

The oven timer sounded and Sally drew a pair of red-gingham oven mitts from her picnic basket and took out the casserole. "It's tuna. I hope that's okay, Meg."

"As long as it isn't covered with potato chips."

Sally looked aghast. "Who would make something like that?"

"My mother. She thought I wouldn't notice the tuna underneath."

"Oh, Meg. I'm sorry. I should've asked if you liked tuna."

"Not to worry, Sally. I enjoy it now. As a kid, no."

"Well, there's enough for Brad tonight, too."

"He's going to be spending the next day or so helping to wind things up relating to the arrest of Wallace Arnhart, so just leave a bit for me."

I placed the salad I'd made on the table, along with a jug of lemonade and some store-bought cookies and we chatted some more about the events of the morning—pausing now and then to congratulate ourselves on our prowess in figuring it all out.

After lunch, Sally took out her notes and cleared her throat. "Time to move on to Arch's death," she said.

We looked at each other, neither of us wanting to be the first to acknowledge the elephant in the room.

"Celeste," we said together.

"There's no getting around it. I hate to think Celeste had anything to do with Arch's death but using our criteria…" Sally said.

"Okay, let's look at Celeste's means, motive, and opportunity."

"Yes," said Sally, "we need to do our 'due diligence.' Perhaps something will occur to us that we haven't thought of before."

"Okay. Means. She's got a medical degree and can write prescriptions, so obtaining the morphine shouldn't be too difficult for her."

"But is that really so?" mused Sally. "She would need to register the prescription, too, wouldn't she? I mean, she wouldn't have drugs lying around in her office."

"Right. Phil Norton said that the FDA has detailed regulations that a prescriber must follow and they must be registered to prescribe certain medications. Doctors are expected not to leave their prescription pads in reach of patients."

Sally took a sip of her lemonade. "So on to motive. Plenty of it, what with Arch taking her savings to fund his gambling habit."

"And leading her on. I wonder if he actually intended to marry her."

"And now she's lost her job—and probably her career. Certainly her position at the clinic she worked so hard to attain."

"And her professional reputation. I wonder what she'll do—assuming she's not found guilty of killing Arch."

"Craig saw her at the train station the other day. Going into the city. Maybe she's interviewing for a position there."

"I hope so. It will be hard for her to get past all this in Bramble, or even in Walnut Creek. I'm afraid there will always be a stigma even if they find someone else to be the murderer."

Sally broke the short silence which followed. "So we've come to the third thing to consider. Opportunity. I understand that it wouldn't take much of the drug to affect him and Celeste had a lot of opportunity without being seen by others—except Arch didn't stay at her house the night before so the Thermos was in his truck the next morning. I think she would've been noticed at the building site."

"What have we got so far?" I asked.

"So far, the best case for having means, motive, and opportunity is, of course, Celeste. Let's look at others that might have wanted Arch dead."

"To start with others who had the means, that's a tough one, given the restrictions and recordkeeping for the drug. So far, there's only Bert who had a prescription for it a long while ago. Arch stiffed him when it came to paying his bill, but Bert didn't seem unduly upset by it. I guess if Bert offered Arch a cup of coffee, he might have had an opportunity to lace it."

"What about Martin Bryson?" Sally asked. "He and Arch were longtime friends. Maybe there's something in the past. Arch stayed with Martin Bryson the night before. But any drink he spiked at his trailer would've killed Arch before he went to work or on the way."

"They're such good friends. It's hard to imagine Martin killing him. And if the motive was something in their university days or when they worked on the pipeline, it's odd that Martin would settle the score years later and in Bramble of all places."

"Who else is there?"

"Well, there's the guys at work," said Sally, making yet another notation. "That whole business with their payroll. I imagine most of those men depend on the money coming in regularly. Rent, car payments, and so forth." She paused. "Although killing Arch wouldn't seem to make a lot of sense. It would further delay resolution of the payroll issue. Unless the intent wasn't murder. It was to scare Arch, which seems a convoluted way to get your paycheck on time."

"I agree. But, speaking of scaring, there are those threatening messages left in his truck. They don't seem to fit with the gangsters running an area gambling operation. A broken kneecap or two would carry a bit stronger message. I suppose street drugs might be easy for them to obtain, but something just doesn't ring true. Arch wouldn't be able to make good on his gambling debts if he was dead."

"That kind of leaves Wallace Arnhart out too. They depended on him to launder their money." Sally put down her pencil. "We've gone over and over all this, but we don't seem to be much further ahead."

I leaned back in my chair and stretched. "There aren't many who had the means—the narcotics—to kill Arch. But, on the other hand, it's hard to identify someone who *didn't* have an opportunity to fiddle with his drink. Just about everyone knew that Arch was a coffee hound. The question is: who hated Arch enough to kill him?"

After another half-hour more of considering and rejecting ideas, we admitted defeat.

After Sally left, I cleaned up the kitchen. Not that there was much to do. Sally managed to add our luncheon things to my already full dishwasher. Reminded me of my college days when we tried to see how many of us could fit inside a VW bug.

Taking a cue from Sally, I decided to write down some ideas about the murder. We were missing something. I closed my eyes and let my mind wander. Means, motive, opportunity? Yes. But there were other things that set my mind astir. What about those threatening notes to Arch? They seemed out of place somehow. What, if anything, did they have to do with the murder? Who wrote them? Block capitals were used by just about everyone—Celeste's signature on her painting, Bert's invoice, Martin's printing on the back of his business card, even George Cadotte's "sold" cards.

My eyes flew open and I sat up. We're looking at all this wrong way 'round. We've been concentrating on the murderer. But what about the victim? Who was Arch? What brought him to our little town of Bramble?

I jotted down what we knew about Archer Donegal. He had an undergraduate degree from Oregon University and held a post-graduate position there while he finished his master's. He was a gifted sculptor, but chucked all that to go to Alaska and work on the pipeline. He was likeable, a brilliant and creative carpenter. And a con man with a gambling habit.

And what about Martin Bryson? It seemed that he was always around and we tended to see him as Arch's sidekick, sort of in Arch's shadow. Like Arch, he held a bachelor's degree from Oregon. He worked as a draftsman. He joined Arch in Alaska to work on the pipeline. They were good friends. When he inherited a mobile home from a relative in Bramble, he moved here and invited Arch to bunk with him. If he had some a grudge against Arch, he certainly wouldn't have opened his home to him or work with him. They worked well together, so after all these months, why wait to kill Arch now?

I doodled a bit more and decided to give up my musings for the day. After almost a full day of sitting, my joints were stiff as I rose from the kitchen table. Mom and Dad had spent most of the day with medical appointments in Chicago and had already turned in. I turned off the light and walked over to the door. The sky was darkening in swirls of mauve and indigo as I ambled down to the pier. A chorus of insects were tuning up for their evening and a slight wind ruffled the surface of the lake. A flash of lightning in the distance promised a summer shower was on its way.

A few fat raindrops began to fall, then increased. I dipped my head against the rain and dashed inside. It was a bit early for me to turn in, but it had been a long day. My string of yawns confirmed it was time for bed. I vowed to avoid thinking about the murder and spend a quiet day at home the next day.

Chapter 31

I woke later than usual, pushed aside the bedroom window curtain, and peeked out. The gauzy film of fog left by last night's rain tempted me to pull the covers up around me and…wait! What was that noise downstairs? Mom and Dad?

I sat up and listened intently, but heard no voices. A scraping sound, like something being dragged across the kitchen floor. And Minerva—where is she? Usually she's swishing her tail in my face to let me know it's past her breakfast time.

Quietly as I could, I slid my feet into my slippers. The rain had cooled the temperature, so the house was too chilly for me to wear only pajamas, so I dug out a sweatshirt from the not-quite-dirty-enough-to-wash clothes piled on the chair. Hoisting my portable hand vacuum cleaner as a weapon—having no baseball bat in my bedroom as they do in TV detective shows—I checked the guest room. My parents were still asleep. I tiptoed down the stairs. The scraping sounds had stopped, but Minerva was in full voice.

I flipped on the light in the kitchen.

The box! Minerva had found the box of Arch Donegal's things that Mom and I had brought home from Martin Bryson's. I'd put it in the pantry and Minerva found it. Like all others of her species, a box was a gift from heaven. She had shoved it across the kitchen floor and was scratching and clawing the box to get into it. The floor was covered with small pieces of corrugated cardboard, and the box—well, it looked like a cat tried to get into it.

Setting down a bowl of Feline Fester on the floor, I distracted Minerva from her yowls of frustration, and picked up the box. It was a bit awkward, but not particularly heavy, so I lugged the box into the dining room where there'd be more room on the table than on the kitchen table that doubled as my work area. I'd forgotten all about the box. I could hardly wait to open it.

I paused to think. In moments like this, I seemed to have a good angel on one shoulder giving me valuable, often dull, advice; and on my other shoulder is another, more adventuresome angel urging mischief.

One thing was obvious. This needed coffee. As I sipped—okay, gulped—my coffee, the two angels whispered in my ears.

It's not your box.

Yeah, but Celeste didn't want it.

That's not quite right; she didn't know if she'd want it. Besides, it's really Arch's box; it should go to his next of kin.

Yeah, but we don't know who that is.

No one's looked very hard for someone.

Yeah, but the box might have stuff in it that would help bring the murderer to justice.

Bring the murderer to justice? Ha! You know you're dying to open that box.

Yeah, you're right. Justice be damned.

I got the scissors from the junk drawer in the kitchen and returned to cut the packing tape and open Arch's box of belongings.

"Margrethe Gae! Just what do you think you're doing?"

Chapter 32

Uh-oh. It was my mother. Using my full name again. She stood, hands on hips, staring at the scissors in my hand. Then at the box. My good guardian angel had called for reinforcements.

"Surely, you're not going to open that box of Arch's things we brought over from Martin Bryson's."

"Um…"

"Meg, that isn't yours."

"It might help us find out more about Arch's death, Mom."

"What does Sally Montrose think?"

"Um…"

"You haven't told about this?"

"She knows we have the box." Drat! If only I'd remembered it when Sally was here yesterday. Although, knowing Sally, she'd probably take the same stance as Mom and my pious angel. "Frankly, I forgot about it until Minerva started trying to open it."

"Well, Meg," Mom replied, a reproving frown forming between her eyes, "it's up to you, of course." Meaning nothing of the kind.

I put down the scissors and asked, "You and Dad are up early. Where are you two going?" Mom was dressed and I heard Dad coming down the stairs.

A furtive look replaced her frown. Mom dropped her eyes and brushed an imaginary bit of lint from her coat. "Um…we're going to meet that nice real-estate agent, Marlene Tigran, for breakfast and look for places to live."

"That's great, Mom." I loved having my folks here with me, but my cottage seemed to get smaller with every passing day. But why her air of secrecy? Aha! After all of her hemming and hawing and fears about meth labs and murderers, I bet they're going to Restful Ponds to look at mobile homes. Not for nothing was I an investigative reporter.

Dad, wearing a sport coat and slacks, came up to us. I gave it another try. "Hi, Dad! Where are you two going all spruced up?"

"Um…" The conversations this morning would not rank among the linguistic triumphs of civilization.

Before Dad could reply—and spill the beans—Mom grabbed his arm and whisked him toward the door. "We'll be late for our appointment. We'd best be on our way!"

"Enjoy the day!" I said to the closed door.

I looked at the box and sighed. Mom was right. Score one for the goody-two-shoes angel. As I headed to the kitchen, Sally telephoned.

"I was just going to call you," I said. "I was wondering if you'd like to drop by a little later."

"How 'bout coming over here instead?" she replied. "Celeste is on her way over, and I thought it might be good for us to talk things over, you know, update her on our thoughts. I'll put some things together for lunch."

"I'll bring the box of Arch's things. Maybe Celeste would like to look through it. I know she wasn't keen on having his stuff, but now that some time has passed…"

"Good idea, Meg. I can always stash the box here if she isn't interested, and the two of us could look through the stuff after she leaves." She paused. "Unless you've already had a look?"

"Of course not!" I replied, as I dropped the scissors back in the junk drawer.

***

Donning my best jeans—after all, I was lunching with the two Bramble fashionistas—I shooed Minerva off the table where she was worrying at the tape on Arch's box. I went into the garage, put down the back seats of my Celica, and hoisted the box inside.

Sally had extended her dining room table with two leaves. It looked almost as long as one of those royal banquet halls; even so, I couldn't imagine Sally and Craig having dinner for two, each of them seated at an end shouting conversation down the length of the table, with footmen at the ready.

At one end of the table were three settings for lunch—white bowls, black napkins, a white tablecloth, and red tumblers for water. A large covered bowl emitted a delightful aroma. Toasted garlic bread and a salad were beside it. The other end of the table was bare except for pads to protect the table. I put down the box there. Presumably, we'd talk after we ate.

Celeste arrived shortly after I did, and after our usual hugs and comments on the weather, Sally led us over to the table. "Something smells marvelous," said Celeste.

Sally lifted the cover from the bowl. "Thank you. I decided to make simple bouillabaisse for us."

"That doesn't look simple to me," Celeste said, peering through the steam from the bowl.

Sally smiled. "Well, that's what Julia Child's recipe calls it. She has a different definition of 'simple' than most of us. By the way, I hope neither of you are allergic to shellfish."

Celeste and I both shook our heads.

"Oh, good. That's a relief. I should've thought of that. Anyway, just put a couple of pieces of bread on the bottom of your bowls and ladle the stew over them. I have some key lime tartlets for dessert," Sally said with a nod to the things on the sideboard, "but I thought we'd have them with coffee as we talk."

***

After we helped Sally clear away the luncheon things, we moved to the business end of the table. By now, I was squirming with impatience. I asked Sally, "Do you have a scissors or something to open the box?"

Sally flashed a look at me that stopped many a chatterer in the Bramble Library. Chastened, I apologized to Celeste. "I'm so sorry, Celeste. What do *you* want to do?"

"No problem, Meg. I couldn't care less about Arch's things before, but now I admit I'm curious. Let's have a look. Although," Celeste laughed and pointed to the ragged tape across the top of the box, "it looks as if someone's been curious about it already."

"Minerva," I said quickly, "my cat. She's never met a box or carton that she hasn't tried to get into."

Sally left and returned with a pair of scissors, some pads of papers, and pencils. "Meg, while she unpacks, let's bring Celeste up to date on our sleuthing—though it's pretty much been unsuccessful so far."

Sally reached for her folder on the table and we began summarizing our discussions from her copious notes of our meetings.

"Wow!" exclaimed Celeste, "you two have been busy." She thought for a while. "So, basically, the motive, means, and opportunity for Arch's murder still seem to be the primary obstacles. I imagine there are pieces missing from what we know of his life." She paused. "And also, what part did the threatening notes he received play in his death? Let's see what's in the box." She stood up, snipped the tape from the box, and began lifting things out and putting them on the table. "I'll set them all out and then we can look through them."

I felt a pang of sadness when I viewed the things she removed and laid before us. So few things to mark a person's life. There were some loose items, among them a couple of paperweights, a small copper rendering of a bear and two cubs, a small box containing studs and cufflinks, and paystubs from the Alaska pipeline company.

Underneath them were several folders containing official-looking items such as his Oregon University diploma, the rental agreement on his former studio, a handful of photographs, and three or four letters addressed to him in Alaska and tied together with rough twine.

We each took a folder or two to peruse. Before we started, we helped ourselves to coffee and dessert, taking care not to spill anything on the box's contents. Just in case, I took a few extra black paper dessert napkins.

The ticking of the mantel clock nearby seemed unnaturally loud as we maintained the vow of silence we'd agreed upon—other than a few surprised exclamations—until all three of us had read and made notes on the items we had from the box of Arch's things. One by one, we put down our pencils and looked up. Sally went over and poured herself a cup of coffee and asked if we wanted a refill. Celeste and I declined, and we began sharing what we'd learned.

Sally sat down. "I'll go first. "I have the jewelry, which is ordinary guy stuff, like cufflinks." She picked up the copper piece. "This looks like his work."

"Yes, I'm sure it is," said Celeste, reaching for it. "It may have been a maquette or model for a larger piece, although it's exquisite as it is."

Sally continued. "He made a lot of money working on the pipeline. No surprises there. The letters, on the other hand, are demands for money."

Sally took a sip of her coffee.

"For heaven's sake, Sally, tell us!" I urged.

"They're from Carina."

Celeste turned white. "The statue!"

"Oh, Celeste," Sally said, giving her hand a squeeze.

"No wonder Arch didn't talk much about his past. I didn't think it could get much worse," said Celeste. He probably ran out on his model, Carina. Martin Bryson had said that Arch went to Alaska to get out of a relationship. That poor woman." Celeste took a shaky breath and urged us to continue.

"Let's see if these photographs tell us anything." I dealt them like a solitaire game on our work area. "Looks like they're all just snapshots, nothing formal." I held one up. "Here's one of a young red-headed girl with pigtails. She and another child have their arms around each other, but the photo's been cut so it shows only the girl. The other child was much younger, judging by the little bit of his or her tanned arm visible." I turned it over. Printed on the back was:

ME AND…AT THE BEACH*!*

The name of the other child was scratched out. But it was enough.

"Sally, do you have the photos you took of the Independence Day store window displays?"

"They're in here with my report." She pulled a dozen or so prints from the sheet protectors in her voluminous binder.

I shuffled through them, found the one I wanted, and squinted at it. "I'll need a magnifying glass."

"I have one in the kitchen. Sometimes need it to read recipes," replied Sally. "I'll get it.

She handed it to me and I held it to the photo of Bushel O'Bargains display featuring George Washington on the Delaware. On the side of his boat was Frieda's campaign slogan:

THE BEST MAN FOR MAYOR IN 2000 IS A WOMAN*!*

"Dear God, Sage wrote those messages!" I said. "Block printing looks pretty much the same, but the italicized exclamation point was the difference," I said as I passed around the photo and the magnifier.

"But, why? Why would Sage send death threats to Arch and Wallace Arnhart?" asked Sally.

"I don't know," I said, "but the notes never did fit in somehow. They had a childishness about them. The dramatic "marked for death" was over the top."

"I bet she defaced Wallace Arnhart's poster, too," added Sally, "although I can't blame her. He definitely was despicable."

Celeste had been quiet all this time. Now she reached for a couple of the paper napkins I'd brought to the table, and began tearing them into small pieces.

Sally and I locked eyes. What was Celeste doing? Had she lost it? Had the stress on so many levels finally sent her over the edge?

Celeste patted the pieces into a neat pile. "Sally, do you have a brochure from the Art Show?"

"Sure." She reached into her folder with her notes and handed a brochure to Celeste.

Celeste put the photo on the table and arranged pieces of the napkins around the little girl's face in the photo, and placed it next to the photo of Carina in the Art Show program. "I saw the resemblance immediately at the Art Fair."

Shocked, we stared at the two images. With the red hair of the girl covered with black, there was no doubt. The girl in the photo was Sage. And Carina must be her mother!

***

"Can I join this group? Maybe I could be a vigil-uncle?" came a man's voice from behind us.

"Craig!" Sally said. "we didn't hear you come upstairs from your man cave."

"I came for some coffee and a couple of those lime things. I confess I eavesdropped on the tail end of your conversation." He looked at the photographs. "I see you've untangled quite a bit. I've been doing some research on my own and have something to add."

He walked over to the buffet table, poured himself a cup of coffee, set two tartlets precisely on a plate, grabbed a couple of napkins, and sat down at the table with us. He sipped his coffee and took a bite from one of the pastries. Good grief, man, tell us what you've found out.

"As you know, I do a lot of international research for various companies and governmental agencies," Craig began. Truthfully, I have no idea what Craig does; I asked him once and he gave me such a detailed and complicated answer, I'd ended up knowing less than I did before and never asked again.

"Brad asked me to look into Arch Donegal's background. There was a bit of a delay because we'd assumed his first name was Archibald, so when I learned his full name—Archer Donegal—I contacted the various companies involved with the pipeline. It was easy from there on. Of course, getting permissions to examine or download private information took some time." Craig took another bite of his tartlet and chewed it thoroughly. I gave an inward scream.

Craig wiped his mouth and continued, "Archer Donegal was married to Carina, and had a child with her—a girl—as you've deduced."

"I thought so, but hoped…" said Celeste. "Was he still married when he was here?"

"No," answered Craig. "Carina died a few years ago. Natural causes."

"But if her mother was sick or in pain for a long time, Sage would perhaps had access to a morphine drug," I commented. "Sorry to interrupt, Craig. Please go on."

"Sage Fletcher is the name she used in Bramble. Her real name is Sagitta Donegal. Because she was paid in cash under the table by Wallace Arnhart, and worked at the hardware store in exchange for lodging, no employment forms or tax deductions from those businesses were filed. However, W-2 wage reporting forms were filed with the IRS and the state from Norton's Drugs and Sundries. With Phil Norton's eyesight failing, Sage did the payroll, along with other tasks that he was unable to do. So her tax forms are under her real name."

Sally said, "My head is whirling. The names: Archer's daughter is named Sagitta, and she used the last name, Fletcher. Wow!"

"What do you mean?" Celeste asked.

Sally responded. "His first name is Archer. Hers is Sagitta, meaning arrow. And a fletcher is one who makes arrows."

Celeste took a deep breath and color began returning to her face. "I've done some investigating too. I contacted a friend, another Art Institute board member, to see if there was something more we could do for Sage. Such a talented young woman, and so friendly and hard-working. She had mentioned something about a scholarship to me. I wasn't aware there was a scholarship for fabric design, and as it turned out, there isn't such a grant. And no one was registered for classes matching what Sage had told us, or had even applied for admission to the Institute."

"So," said Sally, saying aloud what the rest of us were thinking, "What was Sage doing in Bramble?"

Chapter 33

Craig returned to the basement, taking another tartlet with him. The three of us women stared at each other for a long moment, shocked from the possible implications of what we had learned.

Sally was the first to speak. "I can't believe it."

Celeste and I nodded in agreement.

"I hate to say this, but Sage had access to the coffee bar at Norton's. She usually refilled the urns," I said.

We talked for a long while, going over what we learned and sharing ideas. Sally turned to us, and asked, "What shall we do? I know we all think the world of Sage, but I think we should call the police."

"No!" exclaimed Celeste. "Based on my recent experience, I don't have much confidence in Bramble's Finest. Let's contact Brad. He'll know what to do."

"I don't think that's a good idea," I said. "As an FBI agent, he'd be bound to take her into custody."

"Well, we've got to do something," said Sally.

"How 'bout we talk to Sage first? See what she has to say?" I suggested.

"Meg, she may be a murderer. Maybe not on purpose, but she may have come here to talk with her father and it all went wrong," Sally replied.

"I agree with Meg," said Celeste. "Why don't we drop by Fulton's Hardware Store and talk with Sage? We can always call Brad or the police from there." Celeste and I helped Sally take the luncheon things into the kitchen, straighten up the dining room table, and collected our purses.

"We can take my car," said Celeste. "It's blocking Meg's car in the driveway anyway. I need to sell the old Chevy I inherited from my grandfather, so I decided to take one last spin and drive it here. I hope you don't mind, but let's keep the top down. The sun's still out and that breeze is wonderful."

Celeste's "old Chevy" was a classic turquoise and white 1957 Bel-Air ragtop, sporting giant fins and an immaculate interior. A "necker's knob" for driving one-handed was attached to the steering wheel and a pair of fuzzy dice dangled from the rearview mirror. The three of us piled in; I climbed into the back seat.

Celeste backed the car down the driveway, and drove down the street to Fulton's Hardware.

It was almost closing time, but the store was still open so we went over to where Ben was sweeping the store as he prepared to close for the evening.

"Hi, Ben!" I said, opening the door to the sound of its bell tinkling.

"Oh, hi, ladies. You caught me just in time. Just about to close. What can I do for you?"

"Actually, we're looking for Sage."

"She's gone."

Chapter 34

"Gone?" Sally asked.

"Yes. That's why I'm sweeping up—usually her job, you know."

"You mean she's left town?" Celeste asked.

"Yep. She said she received a call from the Art Institute and she needed to go into Chicago for some sort of interview."

"Well, is she coming back, do you know?" Celeste asked.

"No, I'm afraid not. She packed her things and took them with her. Left just a few minutes ago. Called Teddy's Taxi to take her to the station. Said she was going to catch the next train into Chicago." Ben sighed. "Nina and I are really going to miss her. Such a sweet and helpful girl."

The three of us turned and raced for the car, leaving a bewildered Ben Fulton leaning on his push broom and staring after us.

***

Sally looked at her watch. "Ten minutes to six. If we hurry, we can reach the station and catch Sage before the six p.m. train to Chicago leaves!" exclaimed Sally.

We were barely seated as Celeste burned rubber pulling away from the curb. I grabbed the seat in front of me and hung on as we swung around the corner. I leaned forward and shouted to the others, "Chicks and ducks and geese better scurry!" We were going too fast for me to be heard.

We tore down the next street, startling two lake gulls pecking at an empty candy wrapper in front of Norton's Drugs. They scolded us. At least, I think they did. Our car was picking up speed. I struggled to keep my eyes open in the wind and watch Celeste. She looked relaxed in her sunglasses, scarf billowing be-hind her, both hands firmly on the wheel, but her white knuckles and the grim set of her jaw betrayed her ten-sion. Evidently, the car was equipped with power steering, as she easily spun the wheel and we careened around the next corner. Scenes from *Thelma and Louise* flashed before me as we tore through town. I was pinned to my seat; surely, we were approaching Mach 1.

The station came into sight. The clock on the tower showed two minutes before the hour. The train to Chicago was waiting, the conductor looking at his timepiece and indicating to a straggler that the doors were closing. The conductor grabbed the step stool from the pavement and placed it in the train car. The train began to move just as the Bramble's battered cab pulled up. Sage alighted and ran for the train, leaving Ted looking after her. "Hey!" the taxi driver shouted. "My fare!"

Our car's brakes squealed as Celeste stopped the car. Sally leaped from the car and dashed after her. "Sage! Stop!"

Sage turned and looked toward us, but rushed on. She was too late. The last train of the day was gone. Sally and Sage walked back to the car.

I put Sage's suitcase in the trunk as Celeste paid Ted. The four of us climbed into the convertible. Sally and Celeste turned to Sage and me in the back seat. "We need to talk," Sally said. "We can't go back to my house. After our conversation, Craig may have called the police."

"The police? Why?" Sage asked, alarmed.

We ignored her question, knowing it would take more than a quick chat to answer her. I went on. "My parents are at my house, so that's out."

"My place it is then," Celeste said as she started the car. But we didn't move. A police car, lights flashing, had pulled up next to us.

Chapter 35

"Well, well, ladies. Someone called the police station and said that three women were barrelin' down Main Street, headin' toward the train station." Chief Koenig gave the Chevrolet an admiring look as he ran his hand along one of its fins. "Reckon that was you gals." He pointed at Sage. "And, you, missy, are a wanted fugitive from the law."

Before he could compare the scared girl with Richard Speck, I said, as brightly as I could, "Chief, what a coincidence! We were on our way to bring Sage to the police station."

Billy Koenig gave me the fish eye. "Not in this car, you ain't. Dr. Farnsworth here racked up too many moving violations today to drive anywhere for a long, long time."

"I can drive," Sally offered. "Celeste, give me the keys and switch places with me."

"Okay," said Koenig, "but I'm following you. Don't be goin' like a bat outta Hades."

We glided so majestically to the police station, we could've taken Queen Elizabeth along with us to wave to her adoring subjects. In the parking lot, Celeste raised the car's top and we trooped inside to Billy's office.

"Hi, Meg, Sally, Sage!" Brad was already there. "Craig told me about the conversation at Sally's house, so I thought I'd better come in and talk with Billy."

"I'm glad you're here," said Sally. "We…"

"This is a police matter, girls," said Koenig. "Brad's an FBI agent, so he can stay while I talk with Sage. The rest of you girls…"

I clamped my mouth shut. If he called us "girls" one more time, I would have ground my teeth to powder. Celeste spoke up. "I'm representing Sage as her responsible adult," she said. "She's underage and doesn't have a parent or an attorney with her."

"Now look here—" Billy blustered.

Celeste interrupted him. "I'm qualified and licensed to do this. I was appointed *guardian ad litem* for many children I worked with, kids who'd run away from home or had been thrown out by their parents. I was part of a legal team advocating for children under eighteen who were wards of the state during legal procedures. " She paused. "I must call my attorney and have him come over before Sage says one word." She looked at her watch. "It's late, Chief. I'll take Sage home with me. Why don't we all meet here tomorrow morning? Would nine a.m. be okay?"

Billy Koenig gaped and made inarticulate sounds from deep in his throat. Celeste, villainous flaunter of Bramble's traffic regulations, had taken charge. She took Sage's hand and led the procession outside where she and Sage drove slowly out of the parking lot.

Brad drove Sally and me to her house where we dropped her off and I retrieved my car. We agreed to meet the next morning at the police station. Brad began to say something to me about no police guard posted at Celeste's home, then muttered, "I know. I know. It's Bramble."

***

My parents had left a note telling me they were at a movie with their friends from the mobile home park, so I made myself some toast and tea and went straight to bed. Minerva wrapped herself around me and I slept until the alarm clock awakened me at seven a.m.

I was still weary from the activities of the day before, but I staggered through my morning routine and followed the smell of Dad's turkey bacon cooking downstairs. I greeted Mom and Dad, and was overcome by how blessed I was to have these wonderful parents. A tear leaked from my eye.

Mom spotted it right away. "Meg, what's wrong? Sit down, dear." She handed me one of the tissues she always carried in her apron pocket.

Dad put down his *Journal-Times* and peered at me over his reading glasses. "Meg?"

I poured out all that happened the day before.

Dad asked me, "Do you have to go to the police station today? You looked exhausted. I hate to see you put through the wringer again."

"Brad's picking me up—I'll probably stay at his house tonight—and Celeste and the Montroses will be at the station, too. I need to be there for Sage."

"Celeste's lawyer will be there. And the others." said Mom. "You really don't need…" She regarded me. "Oh, never mind. I know that look, Meg. Be off with you!"

***

Brad and I entered the police station right behind Celeste's attorney, Danford H. Chatsworth, Esquire, who held the door for us. "Hello," he said. "I believe we've met before." Smiling with practiced sincerity, he nodded to me and shook Brad's hand. Celeste and Sage were already there. Celeste had done wonders for Sage. Scrubbed of her goth makeup, her hair still black but arranged in a softer look: she looked like the pretty teenager she was. Sally and Craig Montrose came in as we were taking the last of the plastic seats in the lobby. In a few minutes, Billy Koenig, wearing his full police chief regalia, came out to greet us, calling to Chip Kelly, who was manning the desk, to bring in some extra chairs as we followed Billy into his office.

"You all know each other, right?" asked Billy. "So let's get started."

Chatsworth interrupted. He laid a small recorder on the desk. "If you don't mind, I'd like to record this for my client."

Billy, a frown taking up residence on his brow, waved his hand in agreement. "Of course." He turned to Sage. "Now, little lady, you are in serious trouble."

Chatsworth spoke up again, his delivery unctuous as ever. "For the record, let's all introduce ourselves." When we got to Celeste, she introduced herself and the rest of us as part of Chatworth's legal team, noting that Sage was sixteen years old. Celeste must've cleared our presence with the attorney ahead of time, as I can't imagine he would've allowed us in on the conference otherwise.

Billy loosened his collar. He shot an exasperated look at the attorney. "If we're all finished, Mr. Chatsworth, let's begin." He turned to Sage. "As I said, you are in serious trouble. I shoulda held you overnight in a cell."

"In a cell?" Sage turned white. "I did some bad things, but a cell?"

"Those 'bad things' include murder, missy?"

"Murder! I didn't murder anyone!" She looked around the room. "All of you know me. I wouldn't murder anyone!" Celeste reached over and took Sage's hand.

I gestured to Celeste and Sally. "Sage, we've pretty much figured out a lot of it. Arch was your father, wasn't he? And Carina, your mother."

Chief Koenig leaned forward, his mouth worked, but he was poleaxed by this revelation and uttered not a word.

"Yes. I loved her so much. I'm the one who knocked over her statue. I just wanted to touch her, but I didn't feel well…bumped into the table…"

That was it—my uneasiness after I took Sage back to her room at the hardware store: the key cutting machine. "You got into the Community Center because you made a key for yourself, right?"

"Yeah. Mr. Fulton showed me how to make keys at the hardware store, so I made an extra one for myself when I made one for Mr. Bryson. I only made it in case someone forgot theirs."

I continued. "And you wrote the notes threatening death to your father."

"How…?" began Sage.

"The exclamation marks were the same as in the lettering on George Washington's boat in the window display. And the notes were on paper torn off from the roll of butcher paper at the hardware store."

"Okay, I sent the messages. And I also scribbled on one of Arnhart's posters. He was a creep, always finding excuses to touch me. I'm glad he's gone."

Sally said, "Wallace Arnhart will be serving a long prison sentence, Sage. But murder…"

Sage stammered, "I loved my Mom. I don't know why she stayed with my father. I hated him. I'm glad he's dead. But I didn't kill him."

"Sage, we talked about this last evening at my house," interjected Celeste. "We want to believe you. Just tell what you know."

"Mom wrote to my father, asked for money," Sage said. "When she got sick—pancreatic cancer—the doctors at the clinic said there was nothing more that could be done for her. We had no money to pay for anything. A social worker came by to get me to go back to high school. She reported me to someone and they came to our apartment. We didn't answer the door. How could I be gone all day? Mom couldn't take care of Fletch."

"Fletch?"

"My baby brother, Fletcher. Mom thought naming him a stupid arrow name would please my father, but we never sent a photo of the baby to him. He'd know it wasn't his. I did send one of the two of us, but Mom made me cut Fletch out of the picture."

I thought of the child's arm in the photo in Arch's belongings. It wasn't tan from exposure to the sun. It was a Black child. "Fletcher was Martin Bryson's child, wasn't he?"

"Yes." Sage continued. "I called the ambulance, but Mom died on the way to the hospital. A local church had gravesites that were donated, so they gave her one of them. They took care of the funeral and stuff. The social workers brought Fletch and me to the service and took us away right after. They said I was too young to take care of Fletch." Sage glared at us. "How could they think that? I'd been taking care of both him and Mom all that time!"

Sally asked, "Were the two of you placed in a foster home?"

"Yeah, but they separated us. Fletcher cried and cried when they took him, waved to me through the back window of their car." Sage stopped and drew an arm across her eyes. "He was so little. He didn't understand. I tried to find Fletch, but no one would tell me anything, said no one would take a teen-aged girl and a Black child together."

"Sage, how did you end up in Bramble?" I asked. "It's a long way from Oregon."

"Yeah. Mom did write once to Martin. It went to the Alaska job site, then to the hospital where he was.

Someone wrote on the envelope, 'Try Bumble,' but the post office sent it back to Mom. No such place. "I opened the letter after Mom died. She never told Martin about…about his baby."

Celeste reached into her handbag and passed her a package of tissues. "Just take your time, honey."

After a few minutes, Sage continued. "My grandfather really did study at the art colony in Bramble—not Bumble." She smiled weakly. "Mom told me many times that's where I got what she called my artistic talent—from Mom's father, not from Arch. She told me that in private so he wouldn't get mad. So I figured out Martin was in Bramble. Maybe he'd help me find Fletcher.

"I ran away from the people I was placed with. They were okay, I guess. But the kids at the high school made fun of me, my hand-me-down clothes from other foster kids. I just had to get away. I had saved up all the money I got from doing chores around the house, hitch-hiked some…"

At this, the rest of us gasped, imagining the terrible things that could happen to a young girl thumbing rides.

"Oh, don't worry. I only took rides in the daytime from couples and I cut off my hair so I could pass as a boy. I got as far as Walnut Creek and used the rest of my money to take the bus from there to Bramble. I thought it would look funny if I just walked into town from nowhere. The bus stop is there by the hardware store, so I asked for a job there, said I was just visiting for a day or two and staying at the hotel. The Fultons gave me that room and introduced me to Mr. Norton and Mr. Arnhart, so I had a reason to stay." She gave a grin. "And here I am!"

"But the story about…" Sally began.

"Oh, yeah. The Art Institute. Dr. Farnsworth told me last night that she'd found out all about that. I guess I got carried away, too many details—" Sage choked back a sob. "I wanted so much for it to be true."

Chatsworth cleared his throat. "I think that's enough for now, Chief Koenig. Obviously, this girl has done nothing wrong, nothing to prosecute her for. Her pranks were almost justified, given the actions of Wallace Arnhart and Archer Donegal."

"Of course, of course. No problem," agreed Billy. "But that doesn't mean she didn't kill her father. She must've seen him here."

"If I'd known he was here, I never would've come here. I avoided him. He came in to Norton's once when I was filling the coffee urns, but he didn't recognize me. I was just a child when he left for Alaska. I wanted nothing to do with him."

"So you say."

"I didn't kill him!" shouted Sage.

"No, she didn't," came a quiet voice from the doorway. "I killed Arch Donegal!"

Chapter 36

Martin Bryson took a few steps into the office. "I killed Arch. He…"

Brad stood up quickly, moved to Bryson's side, and motioned Martin to take his seat. "I'll stand here by the door," said Brad.

"Don't worry," said Bryson, "I'm not going to try to escape. I can't live with this any longer. I'm sick of pretending how much I liked him. All that crap. And Sage isn't guilty of anything more than a couple of childish jokes."

Celeste spoke up. "I don't think she needs to stay for this. It's been a painful morning already for her." She looked at her watch. "Sage, Sally and I are taking you shopping. And with that, Celeste stared down Billy, took Sage's hand, and marched out. Chatsworth picked up his briefcase and left, with Craig and Sally following closely behind.

We all decided to take a short break. The attorney walked quickly to the exit. Craig gave Sally a peck on the cheek and said he'd see her at home. I asked the two women where they planned to shop.

Sally said, "It's still early. We are going take the train to Marshall Field's and get some new things for you, Sage."

Sage's eye shone. "Field's? I've never been to Chicago. You two are the greatest!" Ah, the resilience of youth.

A troubled look flashed across Celeste's face. Sally must've noticed it too, because she said, "My treat, Celeste." Celeste didn't have enough money to pop for a spending spree.

"Okay," Celeste said, "but let me pay for our lunch then." She linked arms with Sally and Sage and the three almost skipped to Celeste's car. I went back inside.

***

Back in Billy's office, Martin began, "I guess I'd better start from the beginning. Arch and I were at the University of Oregon together and became friends." We all nodded. "Carina was the model for the bronze the university lent us for the art show. For a long time, I didn't know Carina and Arch were married and had a daughter—Sagitta. He thought it was clever: Archer, Sagitta. Arch was never faithful. And even in college, he gambled." Martin's mouth twitched in a slight smile. "He even gambled—and lost—on the pinochle tournament we entered."

He continued. "I ate dinner at their apartment a lot. Usually brought the food since Arch was habitually broke and rarely home. I don't think he was ever violent with Carina or Sage, but he was emotionally abusive, made their lives miserable. Arch was never there, usually off carousing. I fell in love with Carina and…I think it was around this time that Arch became interested in the Alaska pipeline job. He told me he felt trapped and needed to get away."

Martin took a long drink from his bottle of water. "After Arch left for Alaska, I began to look in on Carina and Sage on my way home from work, made sure they were okay, keep them company. I had no idea that Arch had left Carina no money to live on, sent nothing back to her from his wages. She always was bright and cheerful, kind. After Sage was in bed, Carina and I often talked way into the night." Martin brushed a hand across his eyes. "God, I loved her.

"Anyway, I begged Carina again and again to leave Arch. She wouldn't, said she was carrying his child. So…"

Martin looked all of us. "I would've taken care of her and Arch's children. I don't kid myself. It would come with built-in difficulties—white woman, Black man. Racism isn't limited to the Deep South." He sighed. "There was no convincing her, so I decided to join Arch in Alaska. Not sure what my plan was. Maybe keep track of Carina and their kids through him, maybe save up money and try again…I wrote to Carina several times, but she never replied."

None of us said anything. I felt as if I was holding my breath.

"About three years later, a load of pipes slipped as we were unloading them from a semi. Fractured my foot badly; took a couple of surgeries to fix it, and months of rehab at a hospital. Around then, I heard from an attorney that I had inherited the mobile home near Bramble, so I shipped my things, flew to Chicago, bought a used truck, and moved in."

Martin paused, picked at the label on his water bottle. "Then Arch called me. I had lost track of him when I was in the hospital for those months, and, frankly, I wasn't altogether thrilled to hear from him again. I'd put the whole period before Alaska behind me. Or so I thought. I asked him about Carina and their kids, but he always brushed me off. So I dropped it. That was a huge mistake." Martin sighed. "I assumed he and Carina had split up permanently. Or maybe I wanted to think that, you know, that she was okay."

"As you know, Bramble hired Arch and he, in turn, hired me. He stayed with me unless he was with Celeste, which was most of the time. I loved it here. I was accepted for myself, and was content for the first time in a long, long while. Then–" Martin took a long, shuddering breath. "Then, Sage contacted me out of the blue. She was in Bramble. I was at a loss as to what to do.

"She told me Carina had died, and Fletcher was in foster care. Arch had no idea Sage was here. I guess they met once or twice, but he hadn't recognized her. Frankly, I wouldn't have known her either—the goth look, the black hair, and of course, she was a teenager now. I'd no idea what to do. I considered moving somewhere and taking her with me. But a single Black man with an underage white girl—a minor who'd run away from her foster home?

"One day, I was at the hardware store and Nina Fulton asked if I would install a curtain rod in Sage's room. She'd made some room-darkening curtains, and she didn't want Ben on a ladder trying to do it. Sage wasn't there, so it was going to be a surprise for her."

Martin gave a short, humorless laugh. "It was a surprise, all right—for me. I saw the photo Sage had on her dresser: Sage and a little boy, a toddler. The boy was Black. Light-skinned, but Black. I knew right away he was my son."

Martin said, "Fletcher is lost in the system. I've tried to locate him, but they say I have no legal status to claim him. Carina had registered Arch Donegal as the baby's father." He put his face in his hands and sobbed. "If I'd only known…if only I'd stopped by on my way back from Alaska…"

After a few minutes, Brad asked, "What happened next, Martin?"

"Arch and Celeste had a fight and he asked if he could stay with me for a few nights. He was drunk when he arrived and worked his way through the beer in my refrigerator. He sneered about Celeste, called her a cold bitch—the same pattern as his treatment of Carina. Next, he started on Carina, called her a slut, 'probably came on to you, huh, Martin? Bet you wanted to make it with a white gal.' Thank God he didn't know that Fletcher was mine.

"I went for him. I wanted to kill him, but I was no match for him. He was a big guy and he pinned me to the floor. He stood up, grinned down at me, and stomped on my bad foot. I passed out and when I woke up, Arch was asleep on the couch.

"My foot was killing me, so I got out the bottle of pain pills I had left from my surgery and took a couple. That's when I decided to kill him. Arch left cups of coffee all over the job site. Empty, full, old, fresh, hot, cold, whatever. So I took the pills with me the next day and dumped them into one of the cups he left around."

"Weren't you afraid that one of the other guys would drink it by mistake?" I asked.

"I kept an eye out. No one ever touched Arch's cups. Sort of an unwritten rule. And as the boss, he was the only one who had time to drink coffee outside of breaks. I guess we saw it as his 'thing.' The brouhaha with the workers and their paychecks threw me. Never dreamed he would drink the coffee and drive off before…thank God no one else was hurt or killed!"

Brad asked, "Why did you wait so long to confess, Martin?"

"What would happen to Sage if I went to jail?"

***

The four of us left Chief Koenig's office and walked down the hall. Chief Koenig and Martin Bryson turned toward the cells at the rear of the station and Brad and I walked to the front entrance.

In the lobby, Chip Kelly called to me from the front desk. Brad waited while I went over to see what Chip wanted. "Please give Dr. Farnsworth a message. All of her traffic violation charges have been dropped."

"How did that happen?"

"Well, no one from the police force saw her reckless driving—um, alleged reckless driving—and the witnesses said that they couldn't identify the car and passengers after all. Said it might've been a black SUV with tinted windows. They probably figured Dr. Farnsworth had enough to cope with." Chip winked at me. "Tell Dr. Farnsworth she's a free woman."

I looked over at Brad. He shook his head and mouthed to me: "It's Bramble." I laughed. He was well on his way to becoming a true Brambletonian.

***

When we reached Brad's car, he turned to me, cupped my chin in his hands, and said, "Meg, we need to talk. I've accepted an offer on my house, and…well…we need to talk."

Chapter 37

My stomach roiled all the way to Brad's house. Neither of us spoke. Dear God, I've waited too long to tell him how I feel. He gave me so many openings. And now he's leaving. I was determined not to cry and I clenched my hands until my fingernails pinched my palms. What is wrong with me? I love this man and now I'll be stuck in my selfish, independent life. Once inside his house, I sat in the living room while he got a couple of Cokes from the kitchen. I stared at the dark fireplace with its cold ashes.

Brad set the drinks down on the coffee table. My hands were icy and shaking too much to reach for my drink. Taking both my cold hands in his, Brad said, "Meg, I love you. I've loved you since that day when you sported that awful haircut from Gloria's. You were so cheerful about it, and yet I could tell you wanted to go home and stick your head under a faucet. I don't want to live here—or anywhere—without you, Meg. Will you marry me?"

"Yes! Yes!" I was limp with relief and joy and...

He reached in his pocket, pulled out a ring, and slipped it on my finger. "It's a family ring, Meg, but we can go to the jewelry store and you can pick out…"

"Absolutely not, Brad!" I fingered the filigreed setting surrounding a small sapphire. "It's exquisite, the detail…I love it—and you!"

Our Cokes went untouched.

***

"Brad!" I said, admiring my ring as I held up my hand and turned it this way and that. "I need to tell my folks about us. And you should call your parents, your brothers, and…"

"Meg, let's do all that tomorrow. Let's spend a quiet evening here. We can order a celebratory meal from—"

"Not from The Heron. Jon and Louis will tell everyone before we have a chance."

"I was thinking of a fancier take-out for the occasion. How does pizza sound?"

I squeezed his arm. "Sounds right to me."

After dinner, we walked arm in arm to the edge of the lake just as a fish rose out of the water with a splash. "When fish do that, I always wonder what they think of our world. They always return to their home in the water, so I guess they're content with their lives."

"So am I," Brad replied, "I'm content here with you right here in Bramble."

"Speaking of which, tell me about the buyers for your house."

"Well, it's a couple with one child," Brad answered. "They're dropping by tomorrow to take measurements and photos."

Raindrops began to dance on the surface of the water as waves began to lap the shore. Clouds extinguished the stars and we dashed inside as spears of lightning cut through the distant sky. We went back inside, curled up on the couch, and watched the embers in the fireplace wink out. "Brad," I asked, "where will we live when…we're married?" The words were still unfamiliar to me, but so right.

"I was wondering when you'd ask," he said with a smile. "I've put 'earnest money' down on the Podolski house, but if you hadn't said 'yes,' I would've reneged and moved out of Bramble. It wouldn't be the same without you."

I was stunned. "I didn't even know it was for sale. Cam's mother must've persuaded them to move."

"The house was never actually listed. Marlene helped them find a bigger house in Walnut Creek, closer to the hospital. I asked Cam to keep me apprised of their plans. Meg, I'd like us to combine the two houses—yours and the Podolskis'—like Louis and Jon did with theirs. Not as elaborate, of course. What do you think?"

"Oh, Brad. That would be perfect! I know my parents don't want to live in my house—the stairs are so steep for Dad. I think they've been looking at mobile homes, but if not, Marlene will be sure to find them something."

***

The rain storm passed during the night. After Brad and I had breakfast and tidied up for the new owners, I sprayed room freshener around the house. I stepped outside. Canned scent was no match for the after-rain freshness of the morning air and the sparkle of raindrops on tiny, delicate cobwebs in sunlight-suffused grass.

As I came back in, Brad was opening the front door to the couple who bought his house.

Brad said, "Meg, meet the new owners."

"Mom? Dad?"

Brad and Dad high-fived each other and Mom came over and gave me a giant hug. "It's been so hard keeping all this a secret," she said. I sank into one of the chairs, my eyes brimming.

"This guy asked for your hand in marriage. I didn't know men did that anymore." Dad said. The familiar twinkle danced in his eyes. "I, of course, agreed."

"I widened the stairs and put the wiring in for a stair lift. They're coming in a few days to install it," said Brad. "Also a new institutional stove for the kitchen for you, er…"

Seeing Brad floundering, Mom said, "Please call us 'Mom and Dad.' Now, Meg, let's see that ring."

I was too overcome to move while Brad and my parents went through the house, Brad pointing out things while Mom took notes. When they were finished, Dad said, "Time for lunch!"

And Mom, who had inspected the refrigerator soon to be hers, said, "And not left-over pizza!"

We had lunch at The Heron, where Louis and Jon served us champagne and wouldn't allow us to pay for our meal. We swore them to secrecy for the next few hours so Sally, Craig, and the others wouldn't find out via the Bramble grapevine before we had a chance to tell them.

Chapter 38

Brad called his family. Over the phone, I could hear his mother alternately crying and laughing at our news. His father got on an extension, so I "met" his parents for the first time. Chuck and Luke, his brothers, were happy for us and made comments such as, "Finally, old man" and "Does she know she's marrying a dull pencil pusher?" and "So that's the attraction of Bramble." We also called our friends who were delighted.

Mom insisted we sit right down and start making a list of whom we should invite to the wedding. After a few hours, we finally finished—at least, the first draft, until Brad's family sent us names. Brad had begged off—a wise man—but promised to come by later. Mom and I picked up a couple of lawn chairs and walked down to the pier where Dad had escaped. He pulled up his line and turned to face us. "All set for the wedding of the century?" he chuckled "Depending on the date, you have a choice of centuries."

We both laughed and Mom said, "Thank goodness we're having it here in Bramble. This new trend of 'destination weddings' would be a nightmare to plan, and so many people would find it financially difficult to attend. Meg and Brad want a simple reception in the church."

A breeze off the lake whispered the coming of autumn to the trees as they left behind their dark green leaves of summer to change to their annual brilliance. We gazed at the water in silence until the afternoon sun began to fade.

When we got back to the house, the Montrose car was entering our driveway. Sally and Craig emerged, went around the car to the trunk, and brought out a tote bag. As I opened my front door, Sally said, "I brought something to celebrate you finally making a decision about Brad. She stepped inside, grabbed me in a bear hug, and said, "I am so thrilled for you and Brad!"

We went into the kitchen where Sally hugged my parents, and everyone beamed at one another. She opened her insulated tote bag and lifted out several covered dishes and two bottles of Piper Heidsieck Brut. "Cyril Atkins recommended this champagne so I ordered a couple of bottles for special occasions—and this is definitely one!"

"What is that wonderful aroma?" Brad came in the kitchen door. I gave him a kiss and everyone gathered around him with hugs and congratulations. "And champagne!" he said.

I got out a tablecloth and china, we carried our meals into the dining room. After dinner, we moved into the living room with our coffee, and I lit a fire. We watched it dance, the birch logs crackling and sending sparks up the flue.

"This is how life should be," I said.

"And how different from all that happened this year," said Dad. "So many people affected...not to mention that Arnhart guy and the counterfeiting ring..."

"Yes," Sally agreed. "It all came to a head: Arch Donegal and his treatment of women, his gambling addiction fed by Gabe Wright. Sage—that poor little girl thrust into adulthood as she watched her mother's affair with Martin, then caring for Carina as she died. Carted off right after the funeral and separated from her brother. Or half-brother, I should say. The children loved each other. She will need a great deal of professional help going forward. I hope she..." Sally's voice trailed off.

"And the little boy, Fletcher. All alone, taken from the people he loved. Will he ever be reunited with Sage?" said Brad, who paused and added, "Or should he be? I mean, if he finds happiness with another family? When she's older, Sage will decide, I guess."

"Celeste's brilliant career ruined by rumors and opinions of others, 'guilty until proved innocent.' Her love for Arch who depleted all of her savings. And Martin. Such a nice man, so talented. But in love with a married woman. Now a confessed murderer, destined for years and years in prison," I added.

Mom sighed. "Old sins cast long shadows."

Chapter 39

August–October, 1999

Sally dropped by after seeing Sage off to register as a sophomore at Bramble High School. After going through myriad forms and interviews with Oregon officials and our own state bureaucrats, Sally and Craig Montrose were given foster custody of Sage on condition that all of them see a family therapist regularly. "Tom and Todd Winters drove Sage to register for school, and helped her navigate the process. She was both shy and thrilled to be escorted by two senior football players. The twins introduced her to a couple of girls in her homeroom who made plans to meet Sage on the first day of school. I worry about how she will adjust, but it looks like she's off to a good start." Sally paused and gave me a wide smile. "The best news—in addition to you and Brad getting married, of course—is that Sage agreed to have us adopt her!"

"Wow! That's terrific. You and Craig will be wonderful parents. Congratulations!"

As autumn slipped in with glorious colors, Celeste accepted a position at the Chicago Art Institute and moved into a small, two-bedroom apartment in

Lake View *aka* Wrigleyville. She enrolled Sage in a Saturday art class for talented young adults, and when Sage was in the city, she could stay overnight with her.

Unopposed, Frieda Koenig was elected Bramble's mayor, "by a landslide," as her proud husband bragged. She wasted no time in cleaning her official house and issued Chief Koenig his walking papers, or as Billy said, "a golden parachute retirement package." George Cadotte was appointed interim chief of police for a probationary period. Knowing George, I had no doubt he would head up our police force for several years to come. A young associate from Chatsworth, Chatsworth, and Plunk was hired as Bramble's village treasurer after Brad declined Her Honor's offer.

***

In early October, the Week from Hell arrived— moving everyone. We rented a small U-Haul truck, emblazoned with their slogan, "Adventures in Moving." I've always wondered why anyone would want moving to be an adventure; uneventful would be my choice. Anyway, Craig Montrose, Dr. Cam, and Brad drove Celeste and her belongings to Chicago. Mom and her Restful Ponds friends, Gert and Stan, had flown to Arizona the week before to sort furniture and household items to move to my folks' new digs in Cottage Row. Sally and I determined which items from Brad's house would be stored, donated, or tossed. We squeezed his clothing, work items, and other necessities into my guest room. Two vans arrived a few days later—one taking the Podolski belongings to their new home In Walnut Creek, the other bringing my parents' things to Brad's former house. I'm exhausted just listing all of this.

When everything was packed, moved, stored, or unpacked, Brad, Mom and Dad, Gert and Stan, Celeste, the Montroses, and I slumped in near-stupors on Jon's and Louis's deck. We should've bought stock in Bengay. "We're sorry not to have been more help," said Louis. "We've been short-handed, what with Chip Kelly and Barbara Wilcox getting married last week."

Celeste told us that, despite Danford Chatworth's advice, Martin Bryson had pleaded guilty. So there was no jury trial and the judge sentenced him to twenty years in prison. We were silent. Then Mom said, "Like Othello, he loved not wisely but too well."

***

Halloween arrived with a bang. Late that evening, we heard a multitude of explosions coming from across the lake. Sirens wailed. The sky was filled with popping and fireworks, one spluttering "Welcome 2000." Fred Koenig's bargain millennium fireworks had caught fire in the empty warehouse where he stored them in July. We learned later that no one was hurt and that the building was destined to be razed sometime next year. Faulty wiring was determined to be the cause. I imagine there was a verbal explosion that night between Freddy Squared.

Chapter 40

November, 1999

Planning for our wedding until now, had been sporadic. As the date approached, Mom, Celeste, and Sally were galvanized into near-frenzied action. Sally would be my matron of honor, with Celeste as the sole attendant. Brad's older brother, Chuck, would be best man, and his younger brother, Luke, a groomsman.

Craig Montrose dropped by and gave me a five-page, double-sided spreadsheet with a timeline of things to do, listed, literally, to the minute. I thanked him and postponed rolling my eyes until after he left. I vowed to stop—well, okay, limit—my eye rolling. One of these days, they would whirl off into another dimension and drop into someone's living room, along with socks from my dryer and Tupperware lids.

Mom and Sally selected simple flowers for the altar while Celeste made an appointment for me with her hairdresser—assuring me that she'd soothe any of her sister Gloria's ruffled feathers. I held my ground on the subject of a wedding dress—just a simple suit. Celeste and Sally made sure it was in my color palette, whatever that might be. I admit the aqua color and simple lines looked great on me.

Brad and I were busy, too. We picked out plain gold bands at the jeweler's in Walnut Creek. After the wedding, we were going to fly to Denmark to see my Aunt Gae and Uncle Arvid, and from there take a tour through Scandinavia. I would not wear my tea cozy.

We would be gone about two weeks, during which Mom and Dad would stay at my—er, Brad's and my—house and take care of Minerva. Brad's parents would stay in my parents' house, which they'd use as a jumping-off place to visit relatives in the area. Mom and Dad would serve as their guides for trips into Chicago.

On the morning of the wedding, a box arrived for me containing a negligee from Sally and Celeste, along with a card reading: "Don't you dare wear your flannel pajamas tonight!"

***

I thought that after waiting all this time to marry, I would remember every detail. Not so. I do remember cherubic Pastor Joe waiting with the three Trinder brothers at the altar. I also recall Dad's hands shaking as he gave me a kiss and joined my hand with Brad's.

We had dispensed with the usual "bride's side" and "groom's side" of the church, and the four parents sat together. The four of them got along famously. Both mothers dabbed at their eyes and beamed at us.

But the clearest and most indelible memory I have is of Brad and how he looked at me.

The reception was held in what the invitations labeled the church parlors—the new fellowship hall. Brad and I kissed, shook hands, and hugged dozens of friends, neighbors, FBI colleagues of Brad's, and *Journal-Times* friends of mine. Brad and I had attended the retirement party for my editor, Harry Josten, and I was touched to see he'd also come here to wish us well.

I almost didn't recognize Jake Tigran without his red baseball cap. "I burned it," his wife Marlene confided. Across the room, Billy and Fred Koenig talked about the fishing trips they planned to take together. Due, no doubt, to her husband's forced retirement a police chief, Gladys, her lips pressed together in a thin line, was pretending Frieda was invisible. They managed to stay civil at the reception, for which we were grateful.

Millie Pullen was there with her daughter, Charlene, accompanied by a young man she introduced as Paul, her fiancé. Millie said, "Paul is in construction and helped design the Walnut Creek Wellness Center. I'm going to introduce him to the mayor and see if Paul could bid on whatever the plans are for the Community Center."

After Brad and I cut the wedding cake made by Nina Fulton, Phil Norton went over to the microphone. He tapped the mic and asked for the group's attention. He called Brad and me forward and pressed an envelope into our hands. "We took up a collection and this is from all your friends in Bramble," Phil said. "It's okay to go ahead and open it now." Inside was a gift certificate for a generator. "Not very romantic, I know, but we want you to stay here and stay warm for a long, long time." The room rocked with prolonged applause.

Brad pulled me close, and whispered in my ear, "Only in Bramble."

Acknowledgments

With sincere and ongoing appreciation to:

My family and friends, whose love and support strengthen me daily in so many ways;

Readers who have encouraged (and occasionally, nagged) me with inquiries about my next book;

Proofreader extraordinaire, Holly Love.

The Barrington (Illinois) Writers Workshop, whose members cheered me on with their comments and gentle suggestions and corrections.

I am indeed blessed!

About the Author

Julie Kendrick started her writing career contributing articles and short pieces for *The Pitch Pipe,* official publication of Sweet Adelines International. She later served as the organization's International President and is a long-time member of its award-winning Melodeers Chorus.

She also worked as a journalist in the features department of *The Daily Herald* in the Chicago area, and after retiring as managing editor/executive director of the Institute of Environmental Sciences and Technology, she started her own outdoor photography business, Kendrick Photographic Imagery. Julie also edits books of fellow authors and is a popular speaker.

A Long Shadow is the third in the Bramble cozy mystery trilogy. Each book contains a stand-alone plot in the same small-town setting and with the same characters—except those who were murdered or hauled off to jail.

Julie's books are available in soft cover and eBook formats at amazon.com/

www.ingramcontent.com/pod-product-compliance
Lightning Source LLC
Chambersburg PA
CBHW070800120726

47910CB00001B/242